Dark End of Dream Street

Lesley Choyce

⌐

Formac Publishing Limited
Halifax, Nova Scotia 1994

Canadian Cataloguing in Publication Data

Choyce, Lesley, 1951-
    Dark end of dream street

      ISBN 0-88780-296-6 (pbk.)
      ISBN 0-88780-297-4 (bound)

I. Title
PS8556.H668D37 1994 jC813'.54 C94-950291-X
PZ7.C46Da 1994

Formac Publishing Limited
5502 Atlantic Street
Halifax, N.S. B3H 1G4

Printed and bound in Canada

CONTENTS

1

On the Street

I think you're going to get yourself in a lot of trouble," Tara said.

"I don't care," answered Ron. "The school newspaper sucks. What we need is a real paper, something that won't back off and can't be manipulated by the school administration."

It was ten o'clock on Friday night. Other kids were partying or hanging out somewhere having fun, but not Tara and Ron. Ron had been kicked off the student paper for refusing to cover the stories the faculty advisor thought were important. That was the kind of thing that she admired him for. He had the guts to stand up for what he believed in even if he had to pay the price. Yet Tara also knew that Ron liked to get himself in hot water. He loved the attention. And now this, his own underground school paper.

"What are you going to write about?"

"The stuff no one else will print. The truth."

"Truth is relative," Tara countered, ready to start one of their long philosophic discussions about truth. He was the only guy Tara knew who was interested in that kind of talk. She decided he was almost as smart as she was. He was cute too. Sure, Ron had a big ego, but he was the closest thing she'd found to a boyfriend.

"Forget truth, then. I'll just let my writers have the freedom to say whatever they want. Freedom of the press. Freedom to rage if they want to. In fact, that's it. I'll call it *The Rage*. Let the readers figure the double meaning. Popular and outrageous. Hey, there's lots of things to be angry about."

"Who are these writers, anyway?"

"Well, I'll probably do most of the copy for the first issue. Maybe you'll want to do a story."

"Maybe, as long as you promise not to change it."

Ron put his hands in the air. "No way." He smiled. "Freedom of the press. Freedom of the rage."

"What if it's not angry? What if I want to write something upbeat?" Tara looked around at her living room. Plush, comfortable. What did she have to rage about? Maybe other kids had reasons to be angry, like her friend Janet who was always at war with her parents. Tara knew her own life was pretty easy. She got along well with her parents. Sometimes she wondered if maybe it was too good. Compared to Janet's situation, though, Tara thought her life was also a little too tame.

"Come on, Tara. You know as well as I do that we don't get a fair break. Man, kids have no rights at all."

Ron came from a family easily as well off as her own. What did *he* have to be angry about? But he did get angry. He cared about a lot of things — issues like laboratory testing on animals, raising money to fight starvation in Africa. Maybe it was because he was sensitive. Sometimes he was gentle and kind, especially when Tara was feeling low and out of it. But he had built his rep on his attitude. Smart and angry. Not just a goof who got into trouble for skateboarding in the halls. No, Ron was a guy who would take a stand on anything. *Anything.*

The phone rang. Tara was expecting a call from her parents. When they went out for a late night, her father, an administrator at the Victoria General Hospital, would phone to see if he had any calls. Tara's mom stubbornly refused to let him carry a cell phone or a beeper into a restaurant.

"Hello."

"Tara," a breathless voice on the other end of the phone said. "It's me, Janet. I'm downtown. There's this guy..." Tara heard a kind of shuddering on the other end of the phone.

"Janet, calm down. What do you mean? What's going on?"

"This guy. I think he's following me." She was scared, that was for certain, but she also sounded like she might have been drinking or high on something.

"Where are you?"

"Grafton Street, on the corner near the Black Market."

"Are you alone?"

"Yeah. I'm not going back home. I can't."

Home was an on-again off-again thing for Janet. Her family had problems. Big problems. Tara never knew for sure how much of it was Janet, how much of it was her parents.

"What about the guy?"

"I don't know. I've seen him on the street before. He's been watching me."

"Get on the bus. Come straight here."

Ron was looking more than a little annoyed. He knew who was on the other end — Janet. Always in some kind of a fix, always intruding between him and Tara. He couldn't figure why Tara called Janet her best friend.

"Can't," Janet said. "I spent my last dollar on coffee. They had a special on cappuccino at the Mocha Café."

Tara shook her head. Janet had never been known for being practical. Always looking to get bailed out.

"I'm scared," she said.

"Okay. I'm coming. Don't go anywhere. Hang around other people."

"Nobody's around. I think they've already gone to crash at the hotel."

"Don't go there. Stay put. We'll be right down."

The "hotel" was short for what was known as Hell's Hotel, an abandoned building off Barrington where a lot of the kids on the street would crash at night — it was a desperate place for desperate people. Janet had slept there before.

"Hurry," Janet said.

If her father had been home, he probably would have driven them. Instead, Tara and Ron ran down the street and caught the bus downtown. As it was pulling away, Ron threw himself at the door and banged hard. The driver slammed on the brakes and let the two of them on with a look of disgust.

They jumped off the bus on Barrington, ran past Hell's Hotel where they could see candlelight in the top floor windows. As they were running up the street towards Grafton, they saw Janet sitting in the lighted doorway of The Paper Chase. Customers had to walk around her to get in or out. Janet's shoulder-length hair was dyed black and she was wearing a man's trench coat and military work boots — Janet's uniform.

"You all right?" Ron asked.

"Yeah, thanks for coming."

"Where's the goon?" Tara asked.

"He's inside." She pointed to a man, maybe twenty-five years old, who was looking out the window at them while he pretended to be looking through a magazine.

"Why didn't you just go some place else?" Tara asked.

"I figured he'd follow. At least there are other people here."

"Right. Okay. But now let's get out of here."

"Not yet," Ron said. "I think I should confront the creep."

"Not a good idea," Tara told him. "Let's just leave. We don't want trouble."

At least Tara didn't want trouble. Besides, the guy didn't look like he had been hassling anyone.

Ron opened the door and went in. Macho man to the rescue. Tara let go a sigh off resignation. She and Janet followed him inside.

"What's your problem?" the guy said when Ron walked up to him and pulled the magazine out of his hand. There were three other customers in the store along with the woman behind the counter. Everybody stopped and looked.

"I guess I could ask you the same thing." Ron tilted his head sideways towards Janet, who was holding onto Tara's arm like she was scared. Tara glanced at her and decided that Janet was about to start giggling.

"I don't understand," the guy said, sounding as if he was caught completely unaware.

Ron said nothing and clenched his fists. The cashier picked up the phone to call the cops. What she saw was some street kids trying to cause trouble harassing the customers.

The guy watched the cashier speaking into the phone. "Can we go outside, if you don't mind?" he asked Ron.

"Sure," Ron said. "Anything you want."

They walked out and the two girls followed.

"You were hassling my friend here," he blurted out.

"I wasn't doing anything of the kind," the guy said. "Look, I can explain."

"Go ahead, then, explain just what kind of scum you are."

"Look, kid, you got this wrong. You want the real story, give me a minute."

Janet started to laugh a little now — she was either frightened again or high or both. Tara didn't trust anyone right now to keep a cool head. It was up to her. "Ron, let's go."

"Not until I get the explanation." He sounded seriously angry now, the famous Ron Donnelly rage coming to the surface again which Tara knew would make him act like an idiot. Maybe he'd get himself beat up, maybe he'd get all of them in trouble.

The guy was pulling something out of his pocket. Tara didn't like the look of things. What did he have? A gun, a knife?

Ron took a step back.

It was a wallet. "Take it easy," the guy said. "Look, I work for Social Services. This is my job. I spend some time on the street, try to keep on top of the situation. I can't do much but I try to keep kids from getting in really big trouble."

Ron looked at the ID. "This is for real?"

"Yeah, for real. Go in and ask the cashier in there. She knows who I am. It's no big secret but I do try to keep a low profile. I'm not a cop. I do what I can. Call my supervisor if you like. She'll be pretty ticked-off to be woken up, but do it anyway. Look, I wasn't chasing your friend. She looks like a kid in trouble. I was just trying to keep an eye on her so she doesn't end up in worse shape."

Ron seemed deflated, confused. He didn't quite know what to do with all the adrenalin he had just pumped up getting ready to go *mano a mano* with an evil dude of the night. "Kind of like Big Brother watching?" he snapped.

"Something like that."

"Ron, let's go," said Tara.

"I bet you only do it 'cause it has a big fat pay check," Ron kept on the assault.

The guy looked down at his feet, laughed. "You figured me out," he said mockingly.

"Look, we're sorry," Tara said.

"The hell we are. Where does this bozo come off..."

The guy had turned away from Ron and asked Tara, "She got a place to stay tonight?"

"Yeah," Tara said. "She can stay at my house."

"Cool."

Suddenly, Ron was being ignored. He didn't like that, and he didn't like playing the fool either. Before he could say anything else, Tara had tugged him away. Janet was giggling again. "Thanks Tara," she said. "I knew I could depend on you to help me out."

"What happened at home this time?" Tara asked.

"It's kind of a long story."

2

Mirrors Tell Tales

What had happened at Janet's home *was* a long story but it was also a familiar one. It was nearly one o'clock in the morning before Janet got it all out of her system.

"They just don't understand me," Janet said for the fifth time. Tara yawned.

"And you don't understand them," Tara responded.

Ron had gone home, his ego slightly bruised but his mind fired up to write about kids on the street in his new underground paper. Janet was curled up in a sleeping bag on the floor of Tara's bedroom. Tara's parents had come home late and didn't need an explanation about Janet.

"Your parents are so different," Janet said.

"They're all right." Tara's folks were okay. They gave her plenty of freedom and didn't hassle her about her lifestyle. She knew that other kids thought she had it made. "But sometimes I get the feeling that they're so busy with their own lives that they don't have enough energy to really pay any attention to me."

"What are you, crazy? I wish I was so lucky. My mom is always after me about something. Not doing well enough in school, not wearing clothes she approves of. I mean, we argue sometimes for over an hour just about make-up. And my father goes nuts whenever he sees a new boyfriend. I'm fed up. I'm not going back. I need my freedom."

"Be realistic."

"Easy for you to say. But the truth is I'm not going back home."

"Look, Janet, you can stay here for a few days but I don't think you can live here. Where are you gonna go, back on the street?"

"Tara, you've got a part-time job. Can I go with you to the nursing home tomorrow and see if they have an opening? If I can make some money on weekends like you, I can probably find a place to live where I can share the rent."

Tara wanted to just blurt out that there probably wasn't a job at the nursing home and that finding a place to live with some other kids who had left home was going to be a disaster. But she couldn't bring herself to say this. Janet was her friend and that was what mattered.

"Sure," she said. "I'll introduce you to Mrs. Klein. But now we have to get to sleep. I have to be there by eight-thirty."

"Wake me up around six."

"What for? That's way too early."

"I need time to put on my make-up, ya know?"

"Go to sleep."

In the morning, Tara's mom slept in but her dad was in the kitchen making them breakfast. He was cool. He didn't ask Janet anything about last night.

"You girls are up bright and early," he said.

"Janet's going to go see Mrs. Klein about a job."

Mr. Johnson looked at Janet. "Sounds like a fine idea. She can be a little cold sometimes. Don't let it throw you off. She's a good director. Be polite and honest. That's what people appreciate the most at a job interview." He stirred some onions and mushrooms in a frying pan and then poured in some eggs. "You like omelette don't you? It's my specialty."

"Omelette's fine," Tara said.

Tara got her job at the nursing home through her father's connections. She knew that Janet didn't stand a chance of getting hired. They had a waiting list a mile long. Everybody wanted some kind of work.

When the phone rang Mr. Johnson asked Tara to finish cooking. It was probably the first of many calls he'd get that Saturday. Because of his job, he had to be consulted at all hours of the day. Yeah, he was cool but he was always busy.

Knowing that it would be a long conversation, Mr. Johnson addressed Janet as he was walking out of the room. "I know you'll do just splendidly. Be confident. Talk to her like an equal. Good luck." And then he was gone.

They ate the omelette and headed out the door. The nursing home was an easy walk and Janet seemed buoyed up with the enthusiasm that Tara's father had instilled in her. She thought she had the job already. "I feel like my life is finally coming together."

Tara had heard that one before. "Don't count your chickens."

Janet gave her a dirty look. "I'm just being optimistic. I could use a little support."

"Sorry. I'm behind you one hundred percent. I'll give you a good build-up to Mrs. Klein."

Mr. Johnson had made an understatement about Mrs. Klein. "A little cold," wasn't exactly accurate. Janet decided the woman had been carved from a glacier.

Tara had given Janet a very proper introduction as promised. Mrs. Klein had only looked annoyed. *Another one?* Tara thought she could read the woman's thoughts. "I can see you but you'll have to wait. I have a number of responsibilities first."

So Janet waited while Tara went off to her duties, cleaning the rooms of the old people in the nursing home — the "clients" as she was trained to call them.

For the time being, Tara felt good to be free of Janet. She always felt responsible for keeping Janet out of trouble. It was like having a sister but sometimes it felt like a weight around her neck.

One of the great things about working at the nursing home was Emma. And Emma's room was the third one to be cleaned. She was 86 years old, had long grey hair that hung down her back, a face full of glorious wrinkles and eyes that danced. If Janet was the sister she never had, then Emma was the grandmother she had never had a chance to know.

"I can't believe a week has passed by that quickly," Emma said as Tara walked into her room. The sun was shining in through the blinds, lighting up the old woman who was brushing her hair in front of the mirror.

"It seemed like a long one to me," Tara said.

"At any rate, I'm glad you're back. Do you have time to sit and chat?"

"Sure." Tara could spend an hour talking to Emma. She was supposed to be cleaning the rooms but nobody seemed to mind. Some would have called it goofing off but she'd still get her work done, breezing through the other rooms, the ones occupied by people less interesting than Emma. Emma was special.

Tara stood behind Emma and looked in the mirror at the portrait of the two of them. They could have been grandmother and granddaughter — Tara in her clean white uniform and Emma in her soft pink dressing gown. Tara wished it was a photograph. It looked so perfect.

Emma was smiling at her into the mirror. She smiled back. "Mirrors tell you everything, my dear. They tell you what you don't want to know and they tell you what you need to know. And sometimes they tell you this."

By *this* she meant simply the image of the two of them. She held up her fingers as if to make a frame of their image in the glass.

"I'm glad you're here because I need your advice."

Emma turned around and Tara sat down on the bed opposite her. There was an open box of chocolates. Emma didn't eat chocolate. Tara didn't even have to ask. She popped one into her mouth and tasted the sweet richness of it. "Do you want the discount advice or the expensive advice?"

"This is very important. I think I'll go for the deluxe."

"Okay." Tara picked another chocolate from the box and popped it into her mouth. "I'm open for business."

Tara was always happy to give out advice. Janet wasn't the only one who relied on her. Lots of people asked for Tara's opinion and it gave her a tremendous sense of confidence. Even Emma, certainly very wise and experienced, would ask her help in making important decisions and Tara could tell this was a big one.

"My son says I should sign everything over to him. He says that he received the advice from a lawyer. The lawyer said it will make things easier when I die."

"You're not going to die. Not for a long time. You're the healthiest person in this place. I don't even know why they have you in here." Tara didn't want to think about anything happening to good old Emma.

Emma nodded her head. "Well, I suppose. As long as I take my pills." She pointed to an array of bottles on the dresser. There was one to speed up her heart, one to slow it down, one to wake her up in the morning, one to put her to sleep, one to help her breathe better, one to keep the blood thin. The miracles of modern science. "Of course I will be gone at some point. It doesn't matter when. What I need to figure out is what to do about my estate."

"Your son wants you to sign it over to him. Is that what you want to do?"

"I'd like to do whatever makes things easier for him."

"I can understand that. But you said he's not very good with money."

"Never was. But maybe he's smarter now."

"You think so?"

"Well, maybe not. Just a mother trying to think positive thoughts about her son. He's got some debts. Says it wasn't his fault, that there were problems in the stock market that no one could have foreseen."

"And do you think that's why he wants you to sign things over now?"

"I don't know. Could be. But if he needs the money, I should help out."

"Good. Then help out. Loan him what he needs. Don't sign everything over to him. You hang onto it. You're good with money. He isn't. If he can't pay you back, you only lose a little, not a lot."

"I suppose. He'll have the rest when I'm gone anyway, if there's any left."

"Good decision."

"And you're a good friend. Tara, I'm really impressed by how mature you are. Some people are smart but they don't usually have good sense to go along with it. You seem to have both."

Tara didn't know what to say.

"It's important to be in control of your own life, whether you're old or young."

"I know," Tara said. "But it's not always easy."

"What do you mean? Certainly you seem to know what you're doing."

"Well, it's not me. I was just thinking about my friend, Janet."

"Tell me about her."

So Tara proceeded to give Emma the full picture, including the story of last night.

"Well, it was a good thing you came to the rescue."

"I don't know what she'd do if I wasn't around. But she's not going to go home, I know that, and she can't stay permanently at my house. It would drive me crazy. I'm going to try to convince her that getting into some kind of group home might be the way to go."

"Sound's like a fine idea."

Just then Tara caught a glimpse of somebody in the mirror. There weren't just two faces this time but three. And one of them wasn't looking too happy.

"Sorry to intrude," Janet said.

"Oh, hi," Tara said. "How'd the interview go?"

"It was short and not so sweet. She said she wasn't hiring." Janet sounded not just unhappy, but angry.

"Um. Emma, this is Janet."

"I think she knows who I am," Janet interrupted. "You just told her my life's story — your version at least."

Suddenly Tara realized how it all would have sounded to Janet who must have been at the door listening. "I'm sorry. I guess I shouldn't have been blabbing."

"At least now I know how you really feel about me. You with the cool parents, and the good-looking boyfriend, the good grades and oh-so-smart. And me who has nothing."

"That's not what she meant," Emma tried to smooth over the scene.

"That's how it looks to me. And you knew she wasn't going to hire me, too, didn't you?"

"I thought it was worth a try."

Tara suddenly realized that they were both almost shouting. Emma looked very upset and now the figure of Mrs. Klein had appeared at the doorway. She looked straight at Tara.

"We can hear the ruckus from all the way down the hall. What are you two doing in here?"

Janet didn't say a word. She folded her arms and looked smugly at Tara, pleased that she had her revenge by getting her in trouble.

"I'm sorry, Mrs. Klein."

"Seems to me you've upset Emma and we don't like to see our clients put through the wringer like this with a couple of squabbling teenagers. I also think you spend far too much time gossiping with the clients here and not enough time doing your job."

"Now just a minute," Emma said, coming to the defense. "Tara was not gossiping. I was the one who had asked for her help and she was obliged to discuss with me a problem. I don't see that you have a right to criticise her for that. If anything, it was my fault."

Mrs. Klein looked a little miffed. Nobody could get away with talking to her like that except Emma, the one patient in the nursing home who commanded respect from everyone.

"I see," she said abruptly but then, turning to Janet, concluded by saying, "but I don't believe *this* one has a right to be snooping around here. I told her there were no jobs."

Once again Tara had come out unscathed but not Janet. "No problem," she said sharply. "I can tell where I'm not wanted." She turned and walked down the empty hallway, out into the sunlit morning.

3

Wendy's Blues

Tara didn't see Janet again until school on Monday. Janet's parents had said on the phone that she didn't come home on Saturday or Sunday. Tara scoured downtown. Connie, who sometimes hung around with Janet on the street, said she'd seen Janet "around" but Tara didn't have any luck tracking her down. She wanted to apologize for the way things went. Instead of helping her friend, she had ended up causing her more grief.

She ran into Craig in front of the free soup and coffee bus that sometimes parked on Grafton Street. "Maybe she doesn't want you find her," Craig said. Craig had been on the street for a long time. He had problems like all of them but he seemed like some kind of leader. If new kids showed up, Craig was willing to go the distance and make sure they knew where to get free meals, where to bum quarters and where to crash for the night and not get messed up. But Craig had never been too friendly towards Tara. Tara lived the good life. She had it all together, and she sure wasn't one of his tribe.

"Craig, I'm her friend. She needs me. If you see her, will you tell her to call me. Please?"

"I'll be sure to pass on the message," Craig said, his voice flat and insincere. "By the way, about your boyfriend and his little paper, I hope he knows what he's doing. You know, reporters try to write about us all the time or they come down here with their freakin' cameras and start snooping around. They never get it right. They never get the whole story, the real story. They see what they want you to see."

"I think that's why Ron is starting his paper. He thinks there's another side to a lot of things. Did he talk to you?"

"I gave him some good quotes. I hope he doesn't mess with my words."

"Trust him," Tara heard herself saying as she started to walk off. Maybe Ron's intentions were good. He loved to help out at anything he considered a noble cause but she didn't really trust him to get the story straight. He would have his own spin on the whole thing and his own opinions.

On Monday, when Tara finally zeroed in on Janet walking away from her down the hall, she ran to catch up. "You still mad at me?"

"I don't know," Janet said, looking straight ahead. "I get dumped on so often, I kind of get used to it."

"Well, it was stupid of me to be talking like that."

Janet stopped in her tracks. "Tara, no one would ever accuse you of being stupid. Cruel, maybe, but not stupid."

"Whatever I was, I'm still sorry. I don't want you staying mad at me."

"Whatever."

"You know I've been worried about you. Where have you been all weekend?"

"Working things out. Look, you know I can't go back home and I can't stay at your house forever. I guess I just got a little spooked that first night back on the street. But now everything is cool. I got friends there."

"Yeah, friends," Tara said. "But you need a place to live."

"Oh right. Like your bright idea of signing me up again for a group home. Remember last time?"

The last time Janet had allowed Social Services to put her into a group home, she quickly made friends with a couple of kids who were experts at breaking and entering. She learned all about ripping off VCRS and CD players. And then she got busted.

"You just got in with the wrong crowd," Tara said.

"I think I'm better off on my own."

Janet was walking faster now. The bell for class had sounded. Tara felt that a big chasm was opening up between them and she didn't like it. "Janet, okay, I'll stop preaching. I just want to know that we're still friends."

Janet stopped. "Okay, I'll forget about the other day at the nursing home. I'm okay. It was a good lesson. Yeah, we're still friends. Next time, though, let *me* tell my story, all right?"

"Yeah."

But Janet wasn't smiling as she walked into her class. Tara was left alone, feeling confused. She wasn't sure she had patched things up. Tara realized how much she needed Janet as a friend. If Janet had told her to get lost, who would replace her? Tara had to admit to herself that she would have felt really lost, and it would have hurt bad.

Tara needed to talk to someone and she didn't feel like going to math class. She decided to find Ron, find out how his paper was coming. Hadn't she promised to write a piece for it? She wasn't really sure that she wanted to be part of the controversy that was bound to erupt but she had promised. For only the second time in her entire life, Tara decided to cut class. If Ron was in school at all, he could only be in one place, sitting at a terminal in the computer room with some phoney reason for being there instead of in class.

By Friday, according to Ron, *The Rage* would hit the streets or at least the halls of St. Pat's High. And then all hell was likely to break loose.

There was a substitute in charge of the computer room when Tara walked in. She looked up at Tara, waiting for an explanation. Who was she and what was her business coming here after the bell rung?

It wasn't easy to scan the room without standing up on her tiptoes to see over the computer monitors. There he was, in the back, hunched over a keyboard, his face close up to the monitor.

"I'm here to work on my, uh, my project, with Ron." She pointed to him in the back of the room.

"You have permission to be here?" The substitute asked. She was new at this, Tara could tell, and didn't know anything about the rules around the school.

"Of course," Tara said convincingly. "It's a special project for the newspaper." She didn't say which newspaper.

"Okay," the young woman said.

Ron was wearing earphones that were plugged into a tape recorder. He was busy transcribing the tape, crunching away on the keyboard, fast and sloppy, as was his style.

Tara was trying to focus on the words on the screen when Ron noticed her.

"Hey, Tara," he said, taking off the earphones. "How did you like just appear out of thin air?" He hit the brightness control on the monitor and faded the screen to black.

"You should be in English," Tara said.

"And you should be in..." Ron checked his watch, "math. Right?"

"Yeah. But we're both here now."

"That we are."

Tara suddenly had the feeling that Ron was nervous about something, that he didn't want her there. "What are you working on, something for *The Rage*?"

"You got it. It's all coming together great."

The substitute was giving them a dirty look. Tara pulled up a chair beside Ron and decided to whisper. "Maybe I should get a look at what you're including so far so I know what to write about myself."

Ron still had his finger on the brightness control of the monitor, almost as if he was guarding it. There was something on the screen that he didn't want her to see. "Well, you know the whole first issue is only going to be like a four-page tabloid. Space is getting kind of tight. Maybe you should just hold off until the second issue."

Tara felt a little chill run through her. It's true that she had offered to write something because she thought Ron could use some help on the first issue but now what was he saying? That she wasn't wanted.

He read her looks immediately. "No," he said earnestly. "It's not like that. Look, we've established a certain tone to this first issue. It's mostly about kids who get kicked around by the system. It has to be angry and it has to focus on the problem and go right for laying the blame."

"And you're writing the entire issue, just you, right?" Could it be that Ron had to have control over the entire issue by writing everything, she wondered. *What an ego.*

"No, not quite. Look, here's the thing. I've talked to a lot of these kids on the street. I know why they're there. It's like a conspiracy between the parents, the school, the city and the law. It's like they've been shoved out of everywhere and all they have is the street."

"That's a bit simplistic isn't it? You know it's more complicated than that. Tell me how this school encourages kids to end up on the street."

"I'll give you one example. It's in my story. Mr. Henley. Now there's a vice-principal who likes to throw his weight around. Craig says that he was kicked out of here because Henley had it in for him. Craig was caught vandalizing Henley's Toyota. Now that might not have been the right thing for a young scholar to do, but Henley took it personally and he made sure that Craig Hollet got booted from school for good. Henley is part of the system that pushes kids out onto the street."

Tara could see where this was going. "Ron, Henley was responsible for getting you kicked off the school paper. Are you just trying to get personal revenge?"

"What should I do, go scratch up his car instead?"

"You know what I mean. You're not being objective. Isn't that what writing the truth is supposed to be all about?"

Tara knew that Ron didn't like criticism. Ron considered himself smarter than Tara but she knew that he wasn't. And all too often Ron's ego blinded him from seeing the other side of an issue.

"Tara, when this paper comes out, I'm going to get in a lot of trouble."

"Then don't do it."

"I have to. How many kids are down there hanging around Grafton Street without any real place to go. Twenty? Thirty? I owe it to them. I'll get this issue of *The Rage* out and make sure every kid in the school reads it. I'll get myself in hot water and then go to the media. They'll have to take notice of the real story about kids on the street."

"I thought you didn't trust the TV or the papers to report anything fairly."

Ron threw his hands up in the air. "Look, I know I hurt your feelings on this but I don't want you to get into trouble over something I cooked up. That wouldn't be fair." Ron put his hand on her shoulder and brushed back her long hair. He looked straight into her eyes with a warm, genuine smile.

Tara looked away and stared at the black screen of the monitor. Then she reached out and turned the brightness control until the words came up on the screen. At first she didn't recognize the story.

"This isn't your writing," she said.

Ron squirmed uncomfortably in his seat. "I told you, I didn't write the whole paper. I had help. I was just transcribing this."

Tara punched a couple of keys and scrolled the story to the beginning. The title read, "Wendy's Blues."

"Who's Wendy?" Tara asked as she began to read.

"We changed the name. It's a real person but I'll use the pseudonym. It's her story. It needs to be told.

Tara was reading the third paragraph when it clicked. The arguing parents, the group home. It was unmistakeable. It was *Janet's* story. And just like Ron had wanted, the tone was definitely angry, the language was rough — offensive even.

"Everybody's gonna know who Wendy is," Tara said.

"No they won't. I'm not going to tell. Janet gave me permission to use her story. She told me the whole thing. I got it word-for-word on tape. It's tragic but it says it all even better than I could. I'm going to run this as the lead story and then follow up with commentary. The first issue of *The Rage* is going to be a screaming success. It's going to do some serious damage to the system that created this tragedy."

For a split second Tara didn't know whether to hug Ron for being so bloody committed to his cause or to scream at him and tell him he was crazy. She read on down the screen and heard Janet's words echoing in her head, the story that she too had heard before over the many years that they had been friends.

"But what if you're wrong? What if everyone knows this is Janet's story, and what if her language and her accusations here get *her* into big trouble? Remember you told me that Mr. Henley likes revenge and he doesn't exactly come off looking like a saint here. What if this gets her in so much trouble that she gets kicked out of school?"

"That's not going to happen," he said, all too confidently.

"You're wrong. It could happen. It's a real possibility."

Ron studied the words on the screen for a minute, then he looked at Tara. "I guess it's just a chance we have to take."

Tara felt like reaching around and yanking the cord out of the computer, or erasing the file, sparing Janet from seeing her story in print. But she knew it wasn't enough. Ron would persevere. He'd write it again. Ron didn't give up anything he set his mind on. It was one of the things that had attracted her to him, that and his great sensitive eyes. But now she saw this other side of his stubbornness and his so-called compassion and she didn't like the looks of it at all.

She scraped her chair back across the floor, got up and walked out of the room.

4

The Rage Breaks

Tara had to admit that Ron was right about one thing. When the first issue of *The Rage* came out a lot of people noticed. He printed three thousand copies with money out of his own pocket, that is to say, money saved from his allowance. The paper was everywhere around the school and in a bunch of shops downtown.

When Tara arrived at school on Friday morning, she saw Ron surrounded by a crowd of students. She could tell by the look on his face that he was soaking up the attention. When she noticed Carla and her friend, Dionne, doting on Ron, she had a funny feeling in the pit of her stomach.

Tara hung back and Ron came over with a big goofy smile on his face. She knew the paper was his personal triumph and he was on top of the world.

"Whaddya think?" he said, putting his arm around her.

"About what?" she toyed with him.

He pulled a copy of *The Rage* out of his back pocket and held it out in front of her. "The paper, man. What did you think about the first issue? It's hot, I'm telling you. Everybody's onto it."

"I thought you were asking me the question. Or were you answering for me, too?"

"Ooh. A bit touchy, are we?"

Tara found herself bitter with jealousy, but also proud to be, well, his girlfriend. Here was Ron, the centre of attention, just like she was sometimes. Like the time she had led her school debating team to win the provincial championship or when she had organized the school's first battle of the bands. Tara liked to be at the centre of things, too. She was good at making things happen and so was Ron. But now it seemed like he had gone one big step ahead without her. "I found a major typo on page two," she snipped.

Ron threw his hands up in the air. "What? Is that all you can say?"

Tara decided to back off. "Okay," she said. "It was excellent. You captured everybody's attention. But I still wish you hadn't run Janet's story."

"I had permission."

Tara knew that Ron could have talked Janet into anything. Janet's story had made the whole paper. It showed just how easy it was for parents, social workers, and even the school to accidentally "conspire" to push a kid out onto the street. Janet's own words in the paper were simply, "Sometimes there's just nowhere else to go." And so that was the essence of "Wendy's Blues." Put together with the interview with Craig Hollet and a lot of editorializing by Ron and this was a paper with one heck of a punch.

Ron walked Tara to their first period, study hall. If you looked around the room you could see kids reading copies of *The Rage*, but when the announcements came on, all that was about to change. It was Mr. Henley himself reading about basketball practice cancellations and school fund-raisers and the dance on next Friday night. Then he got to the serious stuff.

"We are very concerned about a so-called alternative newspaper circulating at our school. This paper has abusive language and will not be tolerated at St. Pat's. Any copies seen by teachers should be confiscated. If, after today, students are still found reading this paper in school, they may face detention."

Ron was up on his feet. "That's censorship," he said out loud. "He can't do that."

Tara knew that this was just what Ron wanted. There was no stopping him now.

"Will you please sit back down," said Mr. Hader, the study hall teacher. "And be quiet." Mr. Hader was already walking up and down the aisles picking up copies of *The Rage*. If someone stashed it in their school bags, however, before he got to them, he didn't ask them to give it up.

Ron purposefully picked a handful of copies out of his bag and put them on his desk. Tara's first reaction was that Ron was acting like a jerk. He just wanted the attention. All the other kids were looking. She knew she had a choice: let Ron go it alone or become his ally like the old days. It was a decision she wanted to avoid but she did feel a strong sense of loyalty to Ron — for all the time they'd been together and for the fact that he had stuck his neck out.

Tara grabbed a copy from Ron's pile of papers and opened it up, pretending she was reading it, just as Hader got to her desk. When Hader asked her for it, she refused to give it up. When he tried to take it away from her, she held onto the paper until it ripped in half. Tara could read the look in his face: *Don't make me do this*. Tara was beginning to think that she had gotten away with quite a bit in her day because she was one of the smartest kids in the school. None of the teachers liked to see students like her get into too much trouble. Ron, however, was clearly an exception to the rule.

Mr. Hader looked at the stack of newspapers on Ron's desk. "I'll let you have one if you promise to read it," Ron said.

Mr. Hader picked up one, tucked it under his arm. Then when he reached for the rest of the pile, Ron smacked his fist down on top of the papers. "Sorry," he said, "only one per customer."

The full attention of the class was on them now. Mr. Hader was trying to remain calm. "Okay," he said to Ron. "Go down to Mr. Henley's office." Then he turned to Tara and added, "Both of you. Now. Before I lose my cool."

Out in the hallway, Ron said, "That'll be the day. Hader never loses his cool. In fact I don't think the man has any emotions at all. He was manufactured, not born."

Henley appeared to be expecting them. His office door was wide open. "I hope we're not interrupting anything," Ron said. He should have had his classic sweatshirt on, the one that read, "Don't mind me. I'm just a smart ass."

"Sit," Henley said. Tara was beginning to wonder if this was a cause worth fighting for. It was Ron's trip. Sure, she wanted to see something done to help the kids on the street, but the method was all wrong. *The ends justify the means.* She could hear Ron's words echo in her head.

"The issue," Henley began, "is this paper of yours. I don't like something circulating around this school with that kind of language."

"What kind of language?"

"Four-letter words. Foul, abusive words that offend many people."

"If it offends you, don't read it."

"The issue is bigger than that, Ron. The issue is both foul language and distributing lies."

"The issue is freedom of the press," Ron snapped back. This was his scene. If he was going to be a martyr on this one, he wanted to go down in style. Suddenly Tara felt like she had almost been set-up to be there as the audience for Ron's big showdown.

"There are some valid points in *The Rage*," Tara said. "People who run the school and people in government don't seem to understand what it's like out there. Ron's trying to help to change that."

"If I wasn't your vice-principal, I'd probably sue this young man for libel."

"You don't like what I said about the way you treated Craig Hollet?" Ron interjected.

"Craig Hollet has a chip on his shoulder the size of a boulder. It's unfortunate that he pushed us all too far."

"I think it was a personal thing."

"Young man, what you think doesn't matter all that much to me. We need to maintain some sense of discipline in this school and sometimes we have to draw the line. You may think you're setting out to save the world, but I think you don't care who you hurt in the process."

"Who am I hurting — aside from bruising your ego, man?"

"What about Janet O'Brien? Are you sure it's going to help her now that everyone knows her problems. I think you're setting her up for bigger problems."

I looked at Ron. My instincts were right. Henley knew. Everybody knew that "Wendy's Blues" was Janet's story.

"All I did was print the truth," Ron said in his own defense. "And like they say, the truth shall set you free."

Ron was looking pretty smug. He thought he was on top of the world. He didn't care about Janet. He had used her.

"Yeah, my friend. It has set you free. I'm giving you a one week's suspension as of now. As you know, we don't usually do this sort of thing, but I've already discussed the problem with a number of members of the school board. They agree that this could get out of hand, so I have their support. You're free to do something other than come to school."

"That's not fair," Tara blurted out. She wanted to say more but it was hard to come to Ron's defense as she saw him sitting there so satisfied with himself.

"I'm not sure I'm prepared to discuss what is and what isn't fair," Henley said as he turned to Tara. "Now what about you? How do you figure into this?"

"Leave her out of this," Ron insisted, trying to play the macho hero now.

"Should I suspend you as well?" Henley asked Tara. "Am I missing something here that I should know?"

The truth was Tara really didn't want to be suspended. This really was Ron's crisis. Tara knew that a week off would mean missing school work, missing tests, lower grades. She had plans, big plans and that meant she had to finish high school near the top of her class.

"I don't know," Tara heard herself say.

Before Ron could say anything else, Henley told Tara to go back to class.

She and Ron both got up to leave. Tara followed Ron as he walked to the front door of the school. "I guess I rubbed his face in it," Ron said, beaming.

"What about Janet?" Tara asked. "Don't you think it might be tough for her around here now that *everybody* knows all about her problems?"

"No big deal," Ron said. "She'll get over it. Everything will be cool."

Tara wasn't so sure but she knew that what was done was done and some things couldn't be changed. But maybe it was time for Ron to do a little damage control. "Why don't you do a second issue. No heavy language. Maybe print an apology to Henley. He was pretty reasonable, all things considered."

Ron suddenly looked at her like she had just arrived from Pluto. "Are you crazy? I'm holding all the cards and Henley is looking like he's up the creek without a paddle." Ron was out the door. He turned once to say, "Have a nice day in school, sweetheart," and he was gone. For once Tara was really glad to see him go.

5

Guys Are a Whole Lot of Trouble

Despite Ron's attitude, Tara did feel a little disappointed in herself. She didn't like backing down from an issue. Was she wimping out because she was afraid of being suspended, of losing her academic standing?

She opened her locker and looked at herself in the mirror and it became clear to her. This wasn't her problem. Ron had created this for himself, for his own glory. There was a bigger issue here: Janet's troubled life was now public information. Tara was sure this was going to be very bad news. There were girls in school who would taunt her and certain guys who might try to take advantage of her low self-esteem. Janet was going to need her as a friend more than ever and the two of them hadn't even spoken since Monday.

Tara gave herself an insulting look in the mirror. On the surface she looked like she had it all together. Her make-up was perfect, her hair styled just right. But inside she felt like a mess. Why had she not kept in touch with Janet?

She sat through several classes, barely aware of what was going on. When she was called on in English to ex-

plain the meaning of a poem she surprised herself, the
teacher and her fellow students by saying she didn't know
what it meant. All through the day, she asked everyone she
knew if they'd seen Janet. Janet had been around school
this week, but she wasn't around today, the day the paper
had come out.

"She said something about a new guy in her life,"
Tracy Dalloway said. "But that could be all over by now.
Ancient history. You know what Janet's like when it comes
to boyfriends."

Tara knew that Janet had the worst of instincts when it
came to picking guys. She'd chosen some real losers before — guys with drug problems, guys who treated her like
dirt.

"Hey," Tracy added, "I guess you know who the real
Wendy is?"

"Yeah. I'm afraid I do."

"Pretty easy to figure that one out," Tracy said, smiled
and then walked off.

If Tracy knew, then everyone knew, even the ones who
would have had a hard time figuring it out for themselves.
No wonder Janet wasn't in school.

After school, Tara went downtown to Grafton Street,
not far from the public library. Skateboarders were hacking
around the old church, headbangers walking around looking bored, Southend kids trying to look like street kids and
street kids trying to look like they were waiting around for
something important to happen. A whole lot of energy was
stirring around this corner of town without much of a
focus. Kids hanging out.

Sure, Janet had been around. She was always around.
But where? Tara needed to talk to her now.

"I think she's staying with Jake," Craig said.

"Who's Jake?" Tara asked.

"Jake's from Toronto, I think. I don't know much about him. He's new. He's got a place. He let some people crash there before. Girls, that is."

So Tara was beginning to get some sort of picture. "Thanks, Craig."

She turned just then to catch a glimpse of someone walking into the Black Market boutique. Janet.

Tara ran down the street, coming within inches of crashing into a skateboarder trying to do a screeching slide along the curb. Inside the Black Market there was patchouli incense burning, old Doors music, beads everywhere and old hippie clothes like a sixties revival. And there was Janet looking at some kind of a leather hat that she couldn't possibly afford to buy.

"Hey," Tara said softly.

Janet turned. When she saw who it was, she began to head for the door.

"Wait." Tara followed her out into the street. "We need to talk."

"Not much to say. Looks like I've been double-crossed by both you and your boyfriend." She was walking away at a fast clip.

Tara felt strangely abandoned. "He's not my boyfriend!" she shouted to Janet.

That did it. Janet stopped dead in her tracks. No matter what insult Tara had done, she couldn't just walk away without hearing the news, without getting the story. She turned around, slowly walked back to her old friend.

"You two broke up?"

"Not exactly."

"He's a menace, you know," Janet said. Obviously "Wendy's Blues" had already done some damage.

"I think I know that. Guys can be such a pain." Tara wanted to know about this Jake. She didn't want to push it, though. Janet said nothing, looking down at the metal tips of her black army boots.

"Come on," Tara said. "We'll go the Green Bean. I'll buy you anything you like that's on the menu."

"Cool," Janet said.

The café was packed with the high school crowd. They found an empty table by the window and ordered cheesecake and Kenya coffee. Tara didn't say anything until Janet had greedily polished off her plate and was looking a little less frayed.

"I'm sorry about the other day at the nursing home, I really am. That was stupid of me."

"Seems like everyone wants to tell my story. I don't get it. Maybe I can sell the film rights for big bucks."

"Janet, we've been friends for a long time. You have to forgive me."

"You just feel sorry for me, that's all. Everybody feels sorry for me but nobody really wants to help."

"You can stay at my house. For as long as you like," Tara said. "My parents will say it's okay if I insist."

Janet shook her head. "I can't do that to you. Besides, I got a place to stay."

"Jake?"

"How'd you know?"

Tara shrugged, afraid to say the wrong thing.

"Right. Word on the street."

"Tell me about Jake."

"What's to tell. He's twenty and he came down from Ontario. Not bad looking. He saw me hanging around, asked me to come visit. So I dropped by. He was nice. He got a little pushy but I told him to back off and he did."

"And that's it."

"Pretty much. He said I could stay there if I wanted. No strings attached."

"No strings," Tara found herself repeating. Her mind was full of all the worst kind of images. She knew what kind of guys Janet was attracted to and what kind of guys were attracted to her.

"Isn't he a little old?"

"What's age got to do with it?"

Tara decided not to push it on that one. She didn't want to sound like she was prying. She just wanted to be a friend, but there were so many questions in her head.

"You want something else? How about dessert?"

"That's all we had was dessert."

"So. How about another one?"

"Sure. Why not? If you're paying."

"You weren't in school today." There. She said it, sounding all too much like somebody's mother, but she knew Janet wouldn't walk out on her now. Another piece of cherry cheesecake was on the way.

"I don't know if I can face all those kids again. They know everything about me, about my messed-up family."

"Then why did you let Ron do his stupid story?"

"Because he promised no one would know."

"Ron would say anything to get his way."

"But he was so pushy."

"He's pushy all right. He's clever, too."

"You two have a fight?" Tara was suddenly animated. Now *she* wanted the gossip on her friend.

"Not exactly. I just think I've had it with his ego. I think it's over between us."

"You're going to break up with him?"

"I'm thinking about it. I'm just waiting for the right time to do it."

"I don't see how you could ever just drop a guy like Ron. He's got everything: looks, brains, money. You'd have to be crazy."

"Guys are a whole lot of trouble," Tara said and when she looked up at Janet, she saw Janet was smiling. She suddenly felt like they were still two little kids, sharing their innermost secrets. They'd been friends for a long time, through a lot of problems, through plenty of boy-friends.

"A lot of trouble," Janet echoed.

"What about Jake?"

"Jake's okay." Then there was a pregnant pause.

"But?"

"But once in a while, he does have a bit of an attitude."

"What kind of attitude?"

Janet didn't want to answer. "Thanks for the treat," she said. "It's exactly what I needed."

6

Family Photo

So Ron got suspended and Tara watched as he got the glory he craved for. It was election time at school and a normally dull and heartless student council election had turned into something else. Posters started appearing around the halls stating, "Ron Donnelly for President," and "Bring back Freedom of the Press."

Ron wasn't even allowed on the school grounds because of his suspension but Tara knew that he had masterminded this move. It was just like him. But why hadn't he called? That seemed awfully strange.

Henley came on the P.A. Tuesday morning and said that school policy stated that a student on suspension or one with a serious discipline record at the school wasn't eligible to run for a "prestigious position like student council president." Tara knew that he had made that one up on the spur of the moment. No one ever really expected the hard cases to have the gall to run for the office. But Ron was another story.

Right after the announcements there was a line-up of rowdy kids outside Henley's office, shouting, insisting that the vice-principal couldn't get away with this. Strangely enough, a radio reporter from the CBC and a writer from the *Daily News* showed up about the same time. Tara couldn't bring herself to get involved in the scene. She could only marvel at how well Ron had orchestrated all this: first the controversial paper, then getting suspended, then running for student council, now this. The *issue* was no longer helping out kids on the street. The issue wasn't even really something that had to do with freedom of the press. The issue wasn't even how a v.p. could try to manipulate a school election. The issue was Ron Donnelly.

And while all the ruckus was stirring up at school, Ron was probably sitting at home with his CD player cranked up to maximum torque listening to his old Nirvana collection.

In third period, Tara was happy to see that Janet had shown up for English class. Only Janet wasn't looking all that happy to be there.

"What's wrong?"

"I just don't know if I can handle this," Janet said, checking her purple lipstick and make-up as she looked into a pocket mirror.

Tara was trying to lighten her up. "You're not just talking about a boring lecture on poetry are you?" Tara noticed that other students were staring at Janet. She was getting ready to tell them to bug off but the teacher was about to begin.

"I'm talking about them," Janet said, tilting her head towards the kids in the class who were looking at her.

"Don't pay any attention." Tara wanted to add that Janet drew more attention to herself by wearing the outrageous clothes she did — the short leather skirt, the halter top and her combat boots. And that hair — long in the back, shaved on the sides — yikes! But Tara wasn't going to add insult to injury.

"It's not like they even feel sorry for me. It's like they think I'm some sort of geek."

"You're not a geek."

"Great. Get Ron to run that for a headline on the next edition of his stupid paper."

There was nothing more to be said. The teacher was clearing his throat and announcing a pop quiz. "I hope you all know what an oxymoron is."

"Oh, great," Janet said under her breath.

Tara felt really bad for her friend. It was a stupid definition quiz: alliteration, synecdoche, oxymoron, hyperbole. Tara found herself writing the answers in large neat handwriting. She wrote so that her paper was clearly in Janet's view.

Janet was leaning slightly over, trying to take advantage of the opportunity. She started to write but then stopped, let out a very vocal sigh, crumpled her paper up and sat there with her hands up to her face. A couple of girls looked over at her and smirked. Janet pretended she didn't notice.

During the week, Tara hardly ever saw her parents. That wasn't unusual. Her father worked long hours at the hospital. They were in the midst of government cutbacks and he said it took everything in his power to come up with creative ways to keep the place in operation. Janet knew that her father was a good guy, a man who liked to help people. He really cared. Sometimes, she thought he cared too much — about the hospital and the people in it. In her life he had become a ghost.

Hey, but she was Miss Independent. In the eyes of other kids, she had the freedom, she had it made.

Her mom had decided to take up photography. She gave up some of her volunteer work and tagging along with her husband on business dinners. She had always been home when Tara was in elementary school but now that Tara was in high school, her mother said she was "spreading her wings a little." So the walls of the house were covered with dozens of framed black-and-white photographs of super closeups of spider webs and dew on tree branches. She had a particularly haunting photo of Hell's Hotel taken late in the day when the building looked stark, haunting, dangerous. Janet's stories of life at "the hotel" were quite bizarre. Of course, sometimes Janet didn't remember everything that happened. Those were the bad nights when she was hanging out with the dopers or the juice freaks. Looking at the photograph of Hell's Hotel always made Tara think about how close to the edge some people lived, especially her good friend Janet.

There was only one photograph on the wall of her family — the three of them together. It was from last summer at Lawrencetown Beach. Her mom had set the timer on the camera. And there they were, all three of them, together for once, smiling, frozen forever amidst the sand and the sea and the sun. It was near the end of the day. Her father had a sunburn. Her mother had her sunglasses on and was trying to look very casual as the camera clicked. Tara was squeezed between them in the middle — safe and snug.

Her mother said that the "composition" was all wrong. But her father had insisted the photo go on the wall with the rest. He said it was "her best work."

Another Saturday morning, an early breakfast and then off to work at the nursing home. Tara was really looking forward to seeing her old friend Emma.

"You're on your own this weekend," her mother said, making a rare Saturday morning appearance at breakfast. "You don't mind do you?"

"I guess not. What's up?"

Her mother was rubbing her hands together. She was smiling but there was an undercurrent of something. "Your father and I decided to get away for the weekend. We're almost never together. I decided we need some time alone. We're going to White Point Lodge."

Tara realized she should have felt liberated: a weekend alone without parents, the house all to herself. It was something half of her friends would die for, but, instead, she felt a little left out. The camera would click at the beach and the picture would be taken and she wouldn't be in it. "That's great," she said. "I hope you two have a very romantic time."

Her father breezed into the kitchen. "Sorry I didn't make it down for breakfast," he said, kissing her on the head. "You okay Tara?"

"Sure."

"Whatever you need, order out." He left his Visa card on the table. Tara stood up and gave them both a hug and then left for work. She would be alone with her father's credit card and a weekend of freedom.

"Freedom. No parents," she said out loud as she slipped into her uniform in the staff room at the nursing home.

All the while she was cleaning rooms, Tara was envisioning her future. Independence had always been a big part of it. Free to do what she wanted. It was all getting a lot closer now.

When she arrived at Emma's room, she knew Emma would want to hear it all: everything that she was thinking about.

"I missed you," Emma said. She was sitting in her chair, reading a novel.

"How was your week?"

"Like every other week, I suppose, but I can't complain. How is your friend doing? Janet, I mean."

"I think she forgives me. Poor Janet is so used to people dumping on her that she's become used to it."

"Don't give up on her. I bet she's a fine person."

Of course Tara knew that Emma thought everyone was a fine person. She liked everyone and thought the best of people. Tara couldn't understand how she could be so positive about everything.

"I won't give up on her. I just don't know what she's gonna do if I'm not around. She makes such dumb decisions. If I'm not there to help sort out each crisis, I just don't know."

"Well, why wouldn't you be there?"

It was the opportunity Tara was fishing for, a chance to say some things out loud. Nothing ever felt *real* to her until she said it out loud. She knew some things were changing in her life in a big way. "I've been doing some serious thinking," she began. "I think it's mostly because I know it's over between Ron and me."

"You had a fight?"

"No. It wasn't like that." She explained about *The Rage* and then added, "I just want to be more independent, that's all. I'm going to tell Ron it's over. Anyway, I haven't heard from him all week."

"He'll be crushed."

"Nothing can hurt his feelings. Don't worry."

"He is human. Just because he's a boy doesn't mean he doesn't have feelings."

"I'll be gentle," Tara said, but found herself almost laughing. Then she got serious again. "That's just the first step. I mean my parents already think of me as completely grown-up and independent. They left me alone for the weekend. They know I can take care of myself. I'm going to be out of high school in a year and a half. I don't want to go to university right away. I'm tired of sitting in classrooms, and being lectured to. I want to *do* something."

Emma was smiling. "It seems the only time you have to dream your great dreams is when you are young like you or old like me."

"Tell me your dreams."

"My dreams are all about what I once had: a husband, a nice house, good kids. Never thought much about it until it began to disappear. Once you lose your health, all you have left is your dreams."

"But there must have been more."

"Oh, I sometimes wished I could have done other things. Maybe I could have become a doctor, or written a novel. You know."

"Don't you regret that you didn't do those things?"

Emma leaned over. She could have been brushing a tear from her eye. "No," she said. "No regrets. Now enough about me and the past. I want to hear about you and the future."

Tara smiled at Emma. "Well, I want to spend at least a year travelling around Europe and Asia by myself. Just me. That way I have to become part of the culture, not just a tourist. Then I think I'd like to spend some time just living in one place — some place like Nepal or Sri Lanka maybe, just living there and doing what I can do to help poor people."

"I think there are programs set up for young people — Canada World Youth, CUSO. I've known of friends who had kids..."

"No," Tara said, sounding so confident. "I don't want to be part of some organization. I want to do it on my own. I want to see what *I* can do on my own."

"You're much braver than I ever was."

"And then I think I'll go to university, probably in Europe or England, and study everything there is to know about the human mind. My father thinks that the frontier of psychiatry is all tied up in chemicals. Anything wrong with the brain can be fixed with a drug. I think he's wrong. I think there are better methods."

"Those are excellent dreams. I hope they all come true." Emma was standing up now. "You'll have to excuse me but I think I better lie down for a while. I'm so glad you came by. You've absolutely illuminated my day."

Tara helped Emma lie down on her bed. She felt positively recharged by having told Emma her plans. In fact, it was the first time that she had actually put the whole brave tale into words. She knew that it was because of Emma, this amazing person that she could open up to, probably the only person on the planet she could talk to like this.

She could see that Emma was very tired. "Sweet dreams," she said.

As Tara went out into the hall and back to her duties she knew what the very first step in her plan had to be. She didn't want to put it off. There'd be no arguing, no insults, not even any hard feelings. She just wanted to get Ron on the phone and tell him that it was over. She just wanted to be her own person for a while. She wanted her independence.

7

Home Alone

Tara arrived home to a large, empty house at six o'clock. There was a message on the answering machine in her room. It was Ron.

"Hey, I'm sorry I haven't called you sooner. Man, it's been a hectic week as you can imagine. I can't believe I'm going to actually win this student council thing. But look, that's not what I'm calling about. I know I shouldn't do this on a stupid answering machine but, like I say, my life is pretty complicated. I think I better just say this and get it over with. I feel kind of bad about doing it this way..."

There was a pause. The machine cut Ron off with an annoying loud beep. Tara stopped the tape. There was another call on the machine. She figured it must be Ron, part two. She wasn't sure she was ready to hear it. This wasn't the way things were supposed to work out. She knew what was coming next. How could the jerk do this to her?

She got up and walked around her room. She studied her *Star Trek* posters, the plaques she'd been awarded for academic achievement, her old skating trophies, all the little treasures she'd accumulated. When she came to the photo of Ron tucked into the corner of her mirror, she shredded it and threw the pieces around the room, then turned on the answering machine to listen to the rest of the tape. "Look," the big jerk said, "it's me again. I almost chickened out from calling back, but I figure you deserve to hear this. I only want to be honest and fair. Isn't that the way it's always been with us?"

Tara had an impulse to pick up the machine and heave it onto the floor and stomp on it. She resisted. "I just think we've outgrown each other." Ron said. "I think we should see other people. I want us to stay good friends, though."

And that was it. Tara lay down on her bed and looked up at the ceiling. Right then she hated Ron. How could he do this? She couldn't believe her bad timing. She had missed out on dumping him first. She knew that her reaction wasn't logical. It should have been comical. They both wanted the same thing but...

But she got dumped first. Ron had said the words. This was hard to take. It really hurt. She wanted to talk to someone real bad. Why wasn't her mother home, or even her father? They were off doing their own thing.

On a long shot, she dialled Janet's parents' house.

"Sorry, she's not here, Tara. I don't know where she is. You know what she's like."

Tara knew what Janet was like. Screwed up, running from one problem to the next, changing like the wind. Free. Independent. Probably on the street, or with her new loser boyfriend, Jake. Why couldn't she ever listen to Tara's advice? And why couldn't Janet ever be some place that Tara could find her when she wanted to talk?

Realizing that she didn't want to spend the evening alone, she phoned up Carla and then Jessica but they were both out. "What's the use?" she said out loud.

Tara walked downstairs to the kitchen, picked up the credit card left by father and dialled Tomaso Pizzeria.

"What's your most expensive one?" she asked. "Good, I'll have two of them. Delivered."

Tara admitted to herself that she wasn't that hungry. It wasn't the pizza that was important here. She just wanted to try racking up a big bill on her father's credit card. Maybe he'd actually scream at her for this one. Maybe he'd stop being such a nice guy.

Tara survived an evening alone with too much pizza and too many hours watching Muchmusic. It all seemed to blend together into one rap/metal/rock/blues wave of music and commercials except for one really weird video that caught her attention. It was a video called "Beautiful Sadness" by a long-haired poet. In the video he was searching for a woman who was trying to evade him. Then the roles were reversed and he was running from her. In the end, he submerged into this gross pool of green algae and black ooze and disappeared while she rose up out of it and walked away. Really weird. No poetry in English class had been quite like this. The feeling of the song haunted her. How could anyone see any beauty in the sort of sadness that she was feeling? The video only made her feel more sorry for herself. She fell asleep on the sofa.

Sunday morning: work at the nursing home. At least she'd have Emma to talk to. The only problem was that Emma had gone away for the day to visit her son. It was a long, boring and lonely day on the job. Mrs. Klein stopped by to chat but Tara had a hard time being polite. She didn't like Mrs. Klein much, especially after she'd hassled Janet. Tara almost said what she was thinking but had the sense to keep her mouth shut.

As soon as work was over, Tara caught the bus downtown and made the circuit: library, Black Market, Green Bean, The Second Cup, Trident Café, even the hang-outs on Spring Garden Road. Everyone had seen Janet *around*, but not lately. It was a warm evening and a good night just to walk. She went down to the harbour and watched the ferry coming in from Dartmouth. As she watched it pull into the dock, she focused on a figure all in black standing on the top deck. It was Janet. Tara thought this pretty strange. She didn't know Janet spent any time in Dartmouth, across the harbour. Then she noticed a big guy standing beside her: short blonde hair, black leather jacket, a bit of a gut sticking out. Jake?

Tara walked over to the doors to the ferry terminal. She watched as the two of them emerged. The guy went one way and Janet the other. Tara waited a moment then called out, "Janet!"

Janet turned. "Tara. God, it's good to see you." She turned away quickly, looking towards her former companion, checking to see that he was out of sight.

"That's him?" Tara asked.

"That's Jake. What do you think?"

Tara didn't know what to say. Maybe Jake was a great guy. Maybe he just *looked* like a Hell's Angels reject. She shrugged.

"I know. I know. Not a whole lot to look at but he's okay. I've moved in with him."

God no. Here we go again, Tara was thinking.

"In Dartmouth," Janet added. "He's got a little apartment above a tavern on Portland Street."

Tara could just picture what kind of a dump that must be but she kept her thoughts to herself. "I'm glad you're here. I really need someone to talk to."

"*You* need to talk to me."

"Yeah."

"Great. Let's go sit down by the water."

They sat down by the harbour edge, watching the crabs, the fish and the seaweed in the clear water beneath. Tara told her about Ron.

"So what's the big deal?" Janet wanted to know. "You were about to dump him. He saved you the trouble."

Tara wished she could explain exactly why it didn't feel like a happy ending.

"Find another guy. No big deal." Typical thing for Janet to say. Guys came in and out of her life like the tide in the harbour.

Tara was feeling better just being around her friend, just having said what needed to be said. "Tell me about Jake."

"What's to tell. It's not the romance movie of the week but you got to remember whose life we're talking about here. Unlike you, I don't usually end up with the smartest, best-looking guy in the school."

"I'm sorry. It's just that you know I worry about you. I don't want to see you get messed up."

Janet looked up just then, off towards the ferry terminal. "Oh shoot," she said.

"What's wrong?"

"There he is. He's looking for me." Janet got up and pulled Tara along, away from the terminal and towards Privateer's Wharf. As they walked, Tara asked, "What's going on? What are we doing? Why don't you introduce me to Prince Charming."

They had turned the corner of a building now and were standing in an old courtyard with cobblestones. In the middle of the courtyard was a pillory once used to punish criminals. Janet looked like she didn't really want to answer the question. She sucked in her breath and looked back towards the harbour and the gulls soaring above.

"Well?"

"Well, it's like this. Jake doesn't want me talking to you."

"Why not?" Tara felt confused, angry. She didn't know Jake at all but suddenly she felt very hostile towards him.

"He thinks you try to put too many ideas into my head."

Tara had to laugh out loud. It was a laughter of outrage more than anything else. "Janet, you're not going to listen to him are you?"

Janet looked a little embarrassed. She shook her head no. "It's just that this guy feels very protective. He says that if I want to live with him, he doesn't want me out hanging around, you know, doing my own things. He says he doesn't trust the kids back on Grafton Street. He wants to know what I'm up to all the time. He says school is just a bunch of nonsense. I mean, look at what I have to put up with — people staring at me, talking about me, everybody knowing my problems."

"He wants you to quit school?"

"Yeah."

"Janet, don't be crazy. Don't throw it all away." Tara was almost screaming at her. People were looking at them.

"I don't know what to do." Janet had that frantic look in her eyes like a wounded animal.

"I'm sorry," Tara said. "Janet, this guy is trying to control you. That's not right. He can't tell you what to do. Nobody has the right to take you over. Is there more? He doesn't like hit you or threaten you, does he?"

Janet looked at the stones in the wall, then back at her friend. "He doesn't really hit me or anything like that. But he says stuff that really hurts. He makes me feel that if I don't stay with him, then nobody is gonna want me. I'll be all alone." And then she began to cry.

"Janet, you're not alone. I talked to your mother yesterday. She's still mad at you but you can go home if you want."

"I can't."

"Then come stay at my place."

"It would be the end of our friendship. We'd end up hating each other."

"If you stay with Jake, we may never have a chance to stay friends. There is another option. Let's go check out this place called Phoenix House. They take in kids who can't go home."

Janet was shaking her head no. "I can't. I'd hate it." She was trying to stop crying.

Tara saw him first. Jake turned the corner of the building and spotted them. He was walking their way. He pretended not to even see Tara.

"I wondered what happened to ya," he said to Janet.

Janet was trying to pretend she hadn't been crying but Jake could see what was going on.

He looked at Tara and could figure out easily enough who she was. "I thought I asked you to stay away from her," he said to Janet. "What'd she say that made you so unhappy?" When he turned to Tara again, he tried to give her a wordless threat.

"You have no right to control her life," Tara lashed out at him.

"You stay out of it!" Jake snarled, then turning to Janet, said, "Let's get out of here. Let's go home."

"Janet, you don't have to go with him. Come on, I'll take you some place safe."

Jake had his hand on Janet's arm but when he saw the fire in Tara's eyes, he let go. He put his hands up in the air. "Okay, sorry," he said. "Janet, you decide. It's up to you."

Tara wished just then she could reach into Janet's mind and give her strength; she wished so hard she could do something more. Janet looked scared, and shaken. It was a victim's role that she was all too familiar with.

Janet pulled herself together. "It's okay," she told Tara. "It's okay now," and she walked off with Jake, towards the ferry terminal.

Tara wanted to scream. She wanted to stop this from happening but she didn't know how to break the control that Jake had over her friend. She wanted to catch up to them and say that if anything happened to Janet, she would make him regret it. As they walked away, Jake's attitude towards Janet appeared gentle, almost fatherly. Tara knew, though, that things would be different once they were in his apartment. She stood with her fists clenched and pounded them against the stone wall. She felt like there was nothing she could do and maybe she was losing her only true friend. For good.

8

Going Nowhere

When her parents came home from their weekend at White Point Lodge, Tara had an instinct that something was wrong. First, they both hugged her. They hadn't done that for a long time. They had brought her presents — a silver bracelet and matching necklace. What was this? Did they feel guilty for leaving her alone for the weekend? She was sixteen. No big deal. She was dependable. It wasn't like the real-life "Home Alone" couple from Chicago who had gone off to Mexico for a couple of weeks and left their two little kids to fend for themselves.

The pizza boxes were still sitting out on the kitchen table but Tara's mom looked at the mess and said nothing. Tara was hoping her parents would yell at her but they didn't. So she thanked them for the jewellery and asked if they had a fun time.

"Well, we needed the time to talk. I don't exactly know if you could call it fun," her father said.

"I don't get it," Tara said. She looked at her father.

He looked like he was about to answer but her mother spoke instead. "We don't want to talk about it right now. Your father and I still need to work some things out."

"What?" Tara demanded. "What's going on here?"

While her mother headed upstairs, Tara's father put his arm around his daughter's shoulders. "It's no big deal. We'll explain. But give us a few days."

The next morning everything seemed normal at home. The kitchen was all cleaned up by the time she got up. Her father was finishing breakfast and heading out the door. Everybody was spinning off in their own direction as usual. Tara was already worried about Janet, and now she had been left in suspense by her parents.

She made it through Monday but Janet wasn't at school. On Tuesday, she showed up but was as cool as ice to Tara.

Well, at least she knew Janet was okay — more or less. And then Wednesday evening, the bombshell dropped. Both her mother and father were home. That in itself was pretty weird.

"We have to talk," her mother said to her. They all sat down in the living room. Her father clicked the TV to mute but left it on. Ugly images of war in Bosnia covered the big screen TV.

"Just listen to your mother, Tara, before you say anything." Her father was talking in that very calm professional way that he did when he was working at the hospital or talking on the phone to his colleagues.

"I'm going to be moving out," Tara's mom said. "I want you to know that there's nobody to blame. Your father and I don't hate each other. We're still good friends."

"And we both still love you very much," he added.

"What are you talking about?" Tara felt her head fill up with confusion. How could her mother be moving out? Her parents were separating? They never argued, they never fought; they were never together enough to fight or argue.

"I shoulder most of the responsibility," her mother continued, trying to sound calm and rational. "I feel like I'm just beginning to grow. It's partly the photography but it's other things too. I feel like I've never had the chance to have my own life. And I want that now."

"I can understand that," Tara said. "Why do you have to live somewhere else?"

"It's hard to explain. I guess that part of it is that I just need my independence. I'm going to move to Vancouver. I've been admitted into a new photography school. The teachers are some of the best photographers from around the world. I've got an old girlfriend out there who says there are lots of new galleries opening up. She'll help me get established. It's what I always wanted. It's *my* chance to do something. You can understand that, can't you?"

A grey, deadening fog was settling into Tara's brain. "Sure," she heard herself say sarcastically, "I can handle it. I can handle anything." But it was a gigantic lie.

Her father was just looking at the TV screen, the images of Bosnia. "I don't know what to do, Tara. I love your mother very much but she wants very badly to do this. I guess it's partly my fault. I'm not around that much. I haven't been paying attention to what she needs."

"It's something I've been thinking about for a long while but it's been so hard to make this decision," Tara's mother said.

There was that word again coming back to haunt her. "Are you going to get a divorce?"

"I don't know," her mom said. "Right now it's just a separation."

"We'll still be your parents," her father said.

"But what about me?" Tara screamed. "You've figured out what *you* want to do, Mom. But what about me? Where do I fit in?"

Her mom was looking at the floor now. "Oh, Tara. You know I still love you more than anything else in the world," she said, holding back her tears.

Her father cleared his throat. "We've decided it's up to you. You can go to Vancouver with your mother if you like or you can stay here with me. Either way you'll get to visit back and forth."

Tara said nothing. She felt like they hadn't really considered how she would feel at all.

"Look, your mother thought at first we should all just move to Vancouver. There she could get into her photography and I could, well, find a new job. She thought that would be enough for her. But I can't do that. I can't just give up my job, my friends, just give up my career. I can't do that."

"So you decided to split up?"

"Maybe it will just be temporary," her mother said. "I really *need* to try this and it's a once in a lifetime chance. Let me have my try at it and then see. Please try to understand. This is so hard for me."

Tara could not understand why this was happening, why her mother had to go and do this. "I'm staying here with Dad," Tara said. "And that's final."

Tara started for her room but suddenly the whole house seemed alien to her. She didn't want to be around her parents. She hated them. She turned around, and headed for the door.

"Where are you going?" her mother asked.

"Out!" was all she said and slammed the door.

Where was she going? She didn't know. She just started walking. She desperately needed someone to talk to. But who? Ron was out of her life. Janet was living with some gorilla who probably wouldn't even let her in the door. She walked faster but she didn't know where she was going.

All her life, Tara had been the one who had it all together — the good grades, the cool parents, the right answers. People were always coming to her for advice. She'd been lucky. Nothing bad had ever really happened to her. She often felt so strong, like she didn't *need* anyone.

Tonight was different. She kicked at a bottle lying on the sidewalk. She had always been there when Janet or any of the other kids at school had needed her. How come no one was there tonight?

She decided she had to talk to Emma. It wasn't that late. She'd go to the nursing home and Emma would help her sort things out.

The nurse on duty was surprised to see her but, sure, Tara could go down the hall and visit with whomever she wanted to. "Just knock on the door first."

When she came to Emma's room, she knocked but got no answer. She knocked again but nothing. She turned the door handle and went in. The bed was empty. Was Emma in the sitting room watching TV? She said that she hated television. Maybe she was still visiting with her son. That was it.

Just then another one of the nurses walked in. She gave Tara a puzzled look and then recognized her. "Emma had some problems with her breathing," the nurse said. "I think they said it was a collapsed lung. She was taken to Intensive Care at the hospital yesterday."

"How bad is it?" Tara suddenly forgot all about her own worries.

"They say it's pretty bad."

Tara ran out of the nursing home and down the street. She was not used to running. Her own lungs felt like they were burning after she had run for four blocks. Then she came to the hospital, the same one where her father worked. This was the place, she knew, that was the centre of his life — not his home, not his family, but the hospital.

Inside was Emma. She had to see Emma.

The woman at the information desk was not too friendly at first. It was after normal visiting hours and Intensive Care was off-limits to anyone other than family. Emma explained who she was. She was the daughter of Mr. Johnson.

"I'm sorry," the woman said. "Rules are rules."

Tara wanted to say something nasty, something cruel but she said nothing. She went back outside and paced back and forth. From here she could see the receptionist's desk and soon she discovered that about every five minutes the woman went into an office behind her to retrieve files that she was working on. When Tara saw the receptionist get up for the third time, she made her move. She went through the doors, ducked low beneath the desk and soon she was walking down the corridor towards Intensive Care.

Emma's son, the one who had the money problems, was there sitting beside the old woman. Emma was unconscious, lying on her back, a tube in her nose and a monitor tracking her breathing and pulse.

Emma's son recognized Tara. "She's in very bad shape," he said softly. "They don't know if she's going to live."

The words were like hot knives in her heart. "Can I talk to her for a little while?"

The son smiled. "Sure. I'm going to take a little walk around."

When the door closed, Tara sat down beside Emma in the bed. She studied the soft wrinkles in the old woman's face, the long grey hair, the overall gentleness that surrounded her. And she talked. She told Emma everything.

Tara kept expecting Emma to open her eyes, to give her that soft, considerate smile that she had seen every Saturday morning for so many months. They had grown close, very close. Emma had been her link to another time, another generation when life seemed much simpler. Emma had sought Tara's advice, taken it, made her feel like she was wise and important.

"I don't know what to do," Tara said to the unconscious woman. "I wish you were awake to help me. My life is falling apart." Tara remembered how she had shared her dreams with Emma, how Emma had made her feel so brave and confident that she could do anything she wanted. Tonight Tara felt alone and scared. "Emma, wake up, please?"

But Emma didn't wake up. When her son returned, Tara left the room. But she didn't want to go home.

She wandered down to the waiting room, curled up on a chair. There were some worried looking adults in there but she didn't speak to any of them. She started to cry but tried to force back the tears. Her eyes burned. She wanted it all to go away. It had to be just a bad dream. Each time she tried to go back to the room, the attending doctor who she recognized as a friend of her father's, told her that she couldn't go in. "You really should go home, Tara," Dr. Mallory said. "There's nothing you can do here." When it was finally morning, she felt like she had spent the night in hell. She saw Dr. Mallory walking out of Emma's room.

Tara stood up and stopped him. "How is she?"

Dr. Mallory looked her straight in the eye. "She died in her sleep. It was very peaceful. I'm sorry. Come on, let's figure out how to get you home. Does your father even know that you are here?"

"No," Tara said, pushing past him. She ran to the room Emma had been in. She burst in. *The doctor had lied to her.* That was her first reaction. Emma was still in the bed. Her son was not there but two nurses in white were standing beside her. One was removing the tube from Emma's nose. Another was disconnecting the monitor. In a brief, golden, split second, Tara believed that Emma was all better. She was leaving the hospital and going back to the nursing home. She rushed to the bed and made the nurses jump in surprise.

She leaned over. Her heart was pounding in her chest. She focused on the gentle, wrinkled face. Dr. Mallory had not lied. Emma was not breathing.

"I'm sorry honey," one of the nurses said.

Tara started to back out of the room. She felt a cold wave of nausea sweep over her, a profound sense of loss.

Dr. Mallory was there again. "Let's get you home. Please?"

"No," Tara said. She walked past him.

"Where are you going?" he asked, trying to keep up with her as she walked away.

"I don't know," she snapped back. Tara was feeling angry at everyone right then. Even Emma. Everyone had let her down. She felt abandoned.

9

New Image, New Me

Tara walked off down the street. The big question was where to go now. No one close to her had ever died before. How could this be happening to her?

She regretted having left her father's credit card back home in the kitchen. If she had it, she thought, maybe she could just phone up Air Canada and buy a ticket to Europe or Nepal. Any place really far from Halifax. That would have proven to her parents, proven to them all, that she didn't need any of them.

It was a warm day but the fog reached up from the harbour into the heart of the city. Tara usually liked the fog; it gave a soft, fuzzy edge to everything. But today was different. Walking in the fog made her feel more isolated, more alone than ever. She didn't even know where she was going.

She checked her watch and realized it was 8:45. School was about to start. If she couldn't get on a plane and make a getaway, right now, right at this moment, then she decided she would do something completely normal, completely routine, something that would show everyone, or at least herself, that she could handle anything — separation of parents, death, anything. She would simply go to school. She didn't have her homework or her books but what did that matter now?

Wouldn't you know it? There was Ron, right in her path. She had successfully avoided a face-to-face confrontation so far this week after his return to school. Or had Ron been the one avoiding her? He was in the middle of a crowd of students, but when he spotted her, he walked straight towards her.

She needed someone to talk to. Maybe Ron — sensitive, considerate Ron — could help her right now. Then she remembered the message, last weekend, on her answering machine.

"I really hope you're not mad at me," he said, sounding so sincere.

Now Tara was confused. First she wanted to slap him in the face. Just like in the old movies. Slap. *Keep control,* she told herself.

"Mad at you, for what?"

"Well, you know, about my message on your answering machine."

Tara gave Ron a puzzled look.

"Did you leave a message? Oh sorry. My machine's not working. I gotta get it fixed."

She started to go up the steps to the school.

Ron seemed more than a little confused. "Hey wait. Are you sure you're okay? You don't look so good."

Tara touched her hair, realized she probably did look terrible. "Thanks for the compliment," she told Ron. "Now I gotta go."

She had been up all night in yesterday's clothes. She looked bad. When she went into the girls' washroom, she realized just how bad she looked. Her eyeliner and mascara had left black streaks on her cheeks from the tears. Her eyes were puffy and red. As the bell rang she splashed some water on her face and tried clear her head. She was brushing her hair when someone else walked into the washroom. She saw the face in the mirror. Janet.

"Oh my God. What happened to you?" Janet asked. "I've never seen you like this."

Tara didn't turn around. She didn't trust her feelings. The last time they had seen each other, Janet was walking away from her, walking away with a guy who had ordered her not to even talk to her friend again.

"Where's Jake?" Tara asked with a sharp edge to her voice. "Is he standing outside on guard? What's he gonna do if he finds out you've been talking to me?"

Tara turned around. Everyone in her life had let her down. Including Janet. Tara couldn't admit to herself that she was really glad to see her friend.

"Jake's all over," Janet said. "No fun, no freedom. It was as bad as living at home. I'm sorry about the other day. Back then I felt like I didn't have any choice."

Tara smiled. "You really know how to pick a guy."

"Maybe you should give me some pointers."

"Not me," Tara said. "I don't have a clue."

"Poor kid. You're still hurting over Ron."

"I don't know. It's the first time it ever happened to me."

"Is that why you look like this?"

Tara turned to see herself in the mirror again. "No. There's more to it. A lot more." And she told Janet about her parents and then about Emma.

"Wanna cut school, go some place?"

"No," Tara said. "I'm glad you're here. Let's just do school and then we can hang out."

"Okay. But first we have to get you looking human again." Janet set down her huge purse on the sink and started unloading make-up. When they were finished, Tara looked at herself in the mirror. She had on dark eye shadow and a different look to her hair. "It's interesting," she said. It made Tara feel like she had moved one giant step away from her old self. "We look a little like sisters," she said.

"That's cool. Let's go to class."

All day, people looked at Tara a little funny. At first she didn't like it but when she got used to it, she would just stare at whoever it was until they turned away. *New image, new me*, Tara thought. After feeling so strung out she was starting to feel stronger, tougher.

Ron caught up to her at lunch. "Somebody said they saw you tearing down one of the posters."

It was true, Tara was getting sick of the "Ron for President" posters and had torn a couple off the wall when she thought no one was looking. "I put it in a trash can. Don't worry I didn't litter."

"Tara, what's gotten into you? Look, we really should talk. I thought you knew."

Tara liked seeing Ron confused like this. He really did believe that she hadn't heard the message on the answering machine. "Ron, I'm sorry. I don't mean to be cruel but I was thinking last week while you weren't around. I mean, I really need a little more space. I'm tired of always being part of your new project, your new cause." She paused, waiting for the effect. "What I'm trying to say is that I think we should just be friends." Then she turned to walk away.

"Wait a minute!" Ron shouted. "That's not fair. You heard my message on the answering machine. You heard it, didn't you?"

She knew that Ron had a suspicion she had been lying before. But she also knew that Ron wasn't certain. Had he dropped her first or had she just dropped him? He would be pretty sure that he had been tricked. But he'd never know for sure and it would drive him nuts. Tara liked that.

10

Fall into the Void

After school, Janet and Tara checked in at the Café Mocha. It was just like old times. It had been a rough day. She continued to feel a cold ache in her heart every time she thought about Emma. But the way she felt about her parents was another story.

"I want to do something that will make them really mad."

"Hey, you're sitting with the world authority on how to get parents ticked off."

"I knew you could help."

"That's what friends are for."

"Don't tell me yet. Let me bribe you for information first." Tara ordered a couple of slices of Black Forest cake and two espressos.

The plan was simple. Don't call home. Don't go home. Hang out on the street, check into the nightlife, get a little culture, have a little fun.

It was a new feeling for Tara. Six o'clock rolled around and then seven. She'd been away from home for almost twenty-four hours. She hadn't called. She knew her parents would be worried but they deserved it for what they had done to her. She wasn't going to cave in and retreat, not until she'd had at least one night on the street.

Just when Tara felt like they had walked everywhere around downtown and checked out everything, Janet pulled a little bottle out of her purse. She opened it and popped three pills in her mouth, then held out three more for Tara. "Try some. They'll cheer you up."

Tara looked at the pills. She knew that Janet had fooled around with all kinds of drugs that she'd never touch. It was sometimes hard to stop herself from giving lectures on the dangers of this stuff. But that was the old Tara, before her life had been turned upside down. "What are they?"

"Nothing that'll do you any harm."

Tara admitted to herself they looked pretty small, pretty harmless. Right then she decided to trust Janet. After all, Janet was the only one who had remained loyal to her. If she couldn't trust her best friend, who could she trust? She popped the pills in her mouth and swallowed hard.

As it grew darker, more kids appeared on the street. Craig was there as well as a couple of girls Tara had met before. They seemed like a friendly crowd. "I thought things would be pretty dead on a Thursday night."

"Thursday night, Friday night. It's all the same here," Janet said.

Tara started to feel good, real good. Her head felt light and she wanted to laugh. She had been starting to feel tired but now she felt wide awake. She had a tingling sensation in her fingers and the funny notion that her feet weren't attached to the rest of her body.

Janet recognized that her friend was finally high. "What do you think?"

"I think I'm on another planet."

"You are," Janet said. "And wait till you see this."

They walked down Barrington Street. To Tara, all the lights looked like jewels, the people looked almost like they were dancing. Everything looked different and amusing as the street lights lit up downtown. The cars and buses moving down Barrington seemed like exotic giant animals, purring and roaring. "It's a jungle out there," Tara said, then giggled.

They arrived at the Café Olé, a hole in the wall club for kids on Barrington. A bunch of kids in cut-off jean jackets and baggy pants hung out in front of the place. A sign above the door said, "Thursday Night Jam."

Janet seemed to know everyone. Some guys smiled at Tara and she had a hard time not laughing. Everyone looked so funny. It was only a couple of bucks each to get in. Janet was expecting Tara could pay but she was broke, having spent the last of it on cake. Tara felt suddenly very disappointed. She wasn't going to get to go in and hear the music.

"No sweat," Janet said. "Watch this."

Janet walked up to a couple of men in suits waiting for a bus. "Excuse me. Could you help me out with some change. A couple of quarters maybe so I can get something to eat." Tara watched as one of the guys dug in his pocket and gave her some change. She didn't walk away until the other man did the same.

After the bus had pulled away, she said, "Now it's your turn.

Janet had made it look pretty easy but Tara didn't know if she could do it. "I'd be too embarrassed."

"Hey, c'mon. We're in this together, right? Can't expect me to do all the work. Just try it."

Tara took a deep breath as she saw an older woman approaching, steering a path away from the kids hanging out in front of Café Olé. Tara suddenly flashed on the image of Emma lying lifeless in the hospital bed. She pushed the image out of her head. Tara almost didn't know that she had been walking but she found herself standing in front of the woman, right in her path. The woman stopped, clutching her purse in front of her, and looked at Tara. There was fear in her eyes.

"What do you want?" she asked.

Tara now felt very bad about scaring her. "I'm sorry. Very sorry. I just wanted to ask you. Could you, um, spare any money?" She was going to lie like Janet and say it was for food but she couldn't bring herself to do it so she just added, "...for my friend and me."

The startled woman looked at her, relaxed a little, opened her purse and held out a five dollar bill. Tara took the money. "Thanks," she said. "Thank you very much."

As the woman walked on, Tara was swept over with a crazy mix of emotions. At first she wanted to cry. The old woman had been so generous. When Janet saw that she had scored five dollars, she hugged Tara. "Way to go. We're in."

Now Tara felt like a hero — fearless and defiant. "If only my father could have seen that. He'd be totally freaked."

"That's for sure."

They paid the money for admission and walked in just as the lights inside were dimmed to pure black. A band called Good Idea Gone Bad was just about to perform.

Suddenly the stage lights came on very bright and the music exploded in a deafening volume. It was the loudest, craziest, most amazing sound Tara had ever heard. There was a girl on keyboards and a skinny guitar player and a tough-looking character in a T-shirt on drums. The tune really kicked and the kids in the room were dancing as a strobe light flicked on and off making the whole place look unreal.

The music was hard, pounding, and it seemed to take over her mind. Tara knew it was partly the effect of the pills. Her problems were gone; she was lost in the crowd dancing to the music. She tried to focus on Janet in the flashing light. Janet was still there beside her — well, sort of. She was there and then she was gone. There and then gone. The flashing light went from brilliant white to total darkness. During one of the white flashes she saw Janet smiling and knew everything must be okay. Tara tried to relax and let the music take over.

The whole crowd danced and thrashed around, pulsed like some giant amoeba during the slower songs, then jumped around in a frenzy during the heavy tunes. It was a mix of metalheads, skateboarders, street kids and what was left of the grunge scene in Halifax. Tara had never been part of this world before, always a kid on the sidelines, always an observer. Now she was here in the heart of it. She had taken some kind of drug and clearly she'd stepped over the line from respectability. The way she wanted it.

There was no talking. The music was too loud and her ears were ringing. During one particular heavy tune called "Downtown Dangerous" she watched as first one person and then another went up on stage, turned their backs to the crowd and allowed themselves to fall backwards off the stage to be caught by the people below. It looked like some sort of game of total trust. You'd have to trust these people, some friends, some strangers to catch you. Your eyes would be closed, your back to the crowd, you'd fall and, with a little luck, you'd be caught by twenty or thirty hands before you hit the floor.

When she turned to try and say something to Janet, Janet wasn't there. Tara felt a sudden wave of panic. Despite how much fun she was having, she was still pretty stoned. She didn't want to be there alone. "Janet!" she yelled. "Where are you?" But no one answered.

And then she saw her up on stage, back to the crowd. "No!" she screamed out but her frail voice was swallowed up by the drums, the wailing guitar and the sound of the keyboard. She watched as Janet gracefully fell backwards in the most gentle manner. Tara sucked in her breath. Time froze.

And then the crowd of kids up front let out a cheer. Janet had been safely caught and there was another girl on the stage ready to go. Part of Tara's mind relaxed but it was like she had to remind herself to breathe. Her brain certainly was acting strange. She wondered if she had done the right thing by taking those pills. Maybe three were too many.

Then Janet was back beside her, tugging at her to go up on stage. "It's great. You'll love it." She screamed so that she could be heard over the din of the music. Tara let herself be pulled along, her fears gone, infected by the enthusiasm in Janet's voice.

Suddenly there she was, on stage, blinded by the colourful lights now projecting onto her, transported to some other dimension. She stumbled a little, trying to get her bearings. She realized that the crowd in front of the stage was focused on her but she couldn't see any of their faces. She looked at the girl singing and playing keyboards, recognized her as someone who had graduated from St. Pat's last year. She smiled at Tara, gave her a thumbs up.

Tara reminded herself that she had always wanted to go bungie jumping. Maybe this was as close as she was ever going to come. She positioned herself backwards at centre stage with her heels sticking out over the edge. She remembered the first time she'd ever done a back flip off the high dive at Centennial Pool. Beneath her, kids were shouting. Why should she trust these strangers? she asked herself. She could break her neck. The rational part of her brain was telling her this was not a smart thing to do but the drug still made her feel like this was someone else here on stage. It wasn't Tara. She leaned back, closed her eyes and fell into the darkness.

She was floating through clouds. Time slipped into a slow, frozen mode. Drifting, drifting. Then came the cushion of a dozen hands catching her and easing her down to the floor. She opened her eyes. The room was swirling. The music was still washing over her and there were all those faces, smiling, friendly, although some looked pretty hideous in the weird lighting.

She got to her feet and wanted to thank them all for the experience but already someone else was on the stage and she was forgotten.

As she got her bearings and wandered towards the back of the room, she suddenly realized how late it was, how tired she was. She hadn't really had much sleep the night before. She needed to get to bed. She felt like some high-flying airplane about to crash.

Janet found Tara wobbling towards the exit. "I need to go some place to sleep," she said desperately. "I think I'm coming down from the pills. I'm feeling really strange. I need to lie down and sleep."

"You want me to take you home — to your home, I mean."

Tara realized the state she was in, remembered the last words she had had with her mom and dad. No, she didn't want to get into all that. Not tonight. She couldn't go home. Besides it would serve her parents right. They deserved to worry.

"I think I get the picture," Janet said. It was pretty obvious that Tara wasn't going to go home in the condition she was in.

"Where are we going to go?" Tara asked.

"Well, it's not exactly the Sheraton but it'll do."

They walked for three blocks and Tara found herself standing in front of Hell's Hotel. Graffiti was spray-painted on the outside walls. Somewhere upstairs through the fourth-floor windows she could see a faint light.

"Welcome home," Janet said as she led Tara in through the darkened door.

Inside, they tripped over something, recovered, then inched ahead. "The stairs are right over there somewhere," Janet said as they worked their way along the wall.

"I don't know if this is a good idea," Tara said. She realized she was still high. Her mind was working against her, imagining all sorts of horrible things that were ready to jump out at her from the darkness. The place smelled bad and she knew that everything in here was dirty. How could she possibly spend the night in a place like this?

"Relax," Janet said. "I've stayed here dozens of times before. It's very safe."

Just then Tara stepped on something soft. It squealed and sped off across the dark floor. *A rat.* Tara stifled her owns scream. She tried to get control. "Well, at least we're not alone," she said trying to sound brave.

"Don't worry, they're mostly on the first floor."

"Mostly?"

They had found the steps. Tara followed Janet up into the darkness. "I sure hope you know what you're doing."

"Trust me," Janet said.

On the second floor Tara thought she could hear voices, somewhere above. They went up more steps to the third floor. There was an eerie flickering of light on the walls from the street lights outside. It was enough to see that the third floor was strewn with broken chairs and old mattresses. The doors were broken off their hinges. Tara put her hand out and touched the wall and then recoiled.

"I can see where this place got its name from."

"It's not so bad really."

"We're going to stay here?"

"Not here, upstairs."

Only there was no obvious way to get upstairs. The stairway in front of them had been torn down, or maybe it had fallen down.

For no obvious reason, Janet looked up into the empty space where the stairway once stood and shouted out, "Knock, knock. Anybody home?"

Tara couldn't figure out what she was doing or who she was talking to.

But then there was an answer. A guy said, "Who is it?"

"Janet. And a friend."

"Hang on a minute."

Tara thought she recognized the voice. Who was it?

A few seconds later a ladder was lowered. Janet started to climb up but Tara was still having plenty of doubts. She realized there was no turning back. She had come this far so she followed.

In the floor above, a kind of gigantic attic, there were candles burning and kids, fully dressed, lying on mattresses. The welcoming committee consisted of Craig Hollet and a girl he introduced as Charlotte's Web. "She's from Charlottetown and she likes spiders," Craig explained. "What have you guys been up to?"

"Café Olé. Great band. Tara decided she wanted a taste of life outside the comforts of home."

Most of the others were asleep. Craig seemed to be pretty casual about things. Tara was just beginning to calm down and feel a little more comfortable when Craig pulled the ladder back up.

"For safety reasons, you know?"

"Is this place safe?" Tara asked. It was a pretty lame question and she felt foolish as she asked it.

"Depends on what you mean by safe," Craig replied. "It could be worse."

Tara looked at the candles burning, the other kids sleeping on the mattresses. It had seemed like a very warm night but suddenly she felt a chill run through her. Janet led her to a couple of empty mattresses near the window by the street. As Tara lay down on one of them, she realized that her head was spinning around. She had to work hard not to throw up. She didn't know how she had got herself into this. She was scared and she felt awful. She wanted to talk to Janet about it but the room was quiet. The candles had gone out now and everyone had gone to sleep. She was afraid she'd wake someone and she wasn't all that anxious to find out who else was sleeping in this house of horrors — Hell's Hotel. She lay on her mattress feeling cold and sick and wished she could just erase the past week from her life.

She was awakened once in the middle of the night by noises downstairs. Someone was in the building below — it sounded like a couple of men. They were angry and maybe drunk. One of them yelled: "Anybody up there?" But no one answered.

In the dim light, she watched as Craig got to his feet and very quietly crawled to the hole in the floor but just hovered there, silently. They all listened as the two men banged around downstairs, kicking at the walls, cursing, then laughing, then cursing some more. Janet whispered to her, "It's okay. They can't get up here."

After a while the two guys went back downstairs and outside. Tara shivered as she lay there wondering how long it would be before morning arrived, wondering if it would ever arrive. Janet had fallen right back to sleep. But Tara lay there shaking. She didn't know if it was because she was cold or because she was so awfully scared.

11

Parents Deserve to Be Tortured

When Tara woke up she didn't know where she was. As she tried to get her eyes in focus, she wasn't even sure she knew *who* she was. Her head hurt and her mouth felt dry. Then she remembered last night. She remembered the wild excitement of the music. But there was the rest to think about, too. The drugs, the dark journey up the stairs and up the ladder, the noises in the night. Never before in her life had Tara felt so much fear. She wondered how Janet had ever adapted to a life like this.

After the intruders downstairs, she remembered how she finally fell back asleep. She had considered praying for herself. It had been a long time since she had prayed for anything and she had to admit to herself she wasn't sure she even believed in God. So she tried something else. In her mind, she tried to recall the image of Emma while she was alive. Emma who had been so gentle and caring, thoughtful and full of great energy even when she looked weak and old. *So old*. Tara had conjured up the picture and then tried to communicate with Emma. She asked her for help. And now Tara remembered. She was certain that she heard the voice, the voice of Emma inside her head saying that she would be there watching over her, that everything was going to turn out just fine. And then Tara had fallen asleep.

The light of the morning sun filtered in through what was left of the window. Tara surveyed her surroundings for the first time. She looked at the bare brick walls, the bare wood rafters and boards of the roof above. Junk was piled in corners. She saw broken furniture and maybe a dozen mattresses with kids sleeping in various weird positions — stretched out, curled up, some with jackets over their heads.

Craig was awake at the far end, still sitting by the hole in the floor. Tara caught his eye and he smiled. Tara felt embarrassed. Craig understood, said nothing and just looked away. Tara wondered what his story was, what troubles had led him here and how he had become self-designated guardian. Had he stayed awake all night guarding the entrance so that no one could come up? If so, when did he sleep? Tara remembered the article in *The Rage*. Craig had been interviewed but Ron sure as heck had missed his real story.

Janet was awake now. "Hey, we survived," she said.

Tara looked puzzled.

"It was a joke. A little street humour. How does it feel to be among the scum of the earth?"

Tara knew what she meant. In fact, she really did feel like scum of the earth. And she had invited herself to join. "It doesn't feel that good."

"You look terrible."

"You look terrible, too." But it was a lie. Janet looked, well, the same. She had slept in her uniform: her black jacket and tight black skirt, her army boots. Maybe that was the secret to successful street living: heavy make-up, black clothes, army boots.

A wave of nausea swept over Tara. "I gotta get out of here," she said. "Now. I need a washroom and I need some breakfast. I need ... oh God, I don't know what else I need."

"There's a bucket in the corner. And we can order room service if you like."

Tara was amazed at how cool Janet was about this whole thing. Their lives were both being flushed down the toilet and she still had a sense of humour. Another lesson of life on the street. But Tara didn't feel in the mood for humour.

"Can we just get out of here?"

Janet got up and helped Tara to her feet. Other bodies stirred now. Kids peeked out at them from behind unhappy faces. It was only about eight o'clock. Apparently the other campers were used to sleeping in late.

Craig said nothing at all. He let the ladder down. When they were safely on the floor below, he said "See ya," and pulled the ladder back up. Tara had been thinking about something: hell. It had been up, not down. And she had survived it. Survived it once. "I don't think I ever want to do that again."

"That's okay. You have a choice. Some of us don't."

"I don't see how you can say that," Tara said.

"You haven't lived my life."

Tara wasn't in the mood to give Janet a lecture. She was feeling kind of edgy. Was it something left over from the drug or was she mad at her friend for getting her into last night? "I could really use a coffee and a croissant," Tara said.

"Croissant?" Janet said. "Give me a break. As you might recall we're a little short on funds."

"Oh yeah."

"But we can always beg."

"Right." Tara said. But she wasn't in the mood to stop people and ask for hand-outs. Last night was different. She was high. But now she was straight, very straight and she looked like something the cat dragged in. "I can't do it."

Janet gave her a look of disgust, then shrugged, took a deep breath and went over to the first person coming her way, a guy with a briefcase hurrying to his office. " 'Scuse me sir. My friend over there was wondering if you might have some spare change for a croissant."

He kept on going. The guy looked at Tara though and just shook his head. Janet tried a second time and then a third. By the fourth try, she got a quarter, then someone offered up a dollar. Tara just stood there, feeling more and more uncomfortable.

Finally Janet spoke to her. "We got enough to split a coffee and a croissant. But you'll owe me one."

"I'll pay you back with interest." In truth, Tara had bought Janet a lot of coffee and food over the years. If she had been counting, Janet would have run up a pretty healthy tab. But all that was in the past. Janet had just paid her back double.

In the washroom at Tim Horton's, Tara tried to make the damage look minimal. Her hair was a rat's nest; her face looked pale and sickly. Her clothes looked like she had, well, slept in them. It wasn't a pretty picture but she tried to cover the damage with fresh make-up and she brushed the barbed-wire knots out of her hair.

When she sat back down she noticed that Janet had ordered. She had her croissant — a whole one sitting on a plate for Tara. Janet was eating toast with marmalade and she had half of a donut in front of her.

"I don't get it."

"The people at the next table over. Real slobs. They left half their food on the plate. I figured it was only going to get chucked so I saved the waitress some work." She bit into the donut and wiped the white sugar powder off her lips.

Tara ate the croissant and thanked her friend again.

"What would your parents think, Tara, about last night?"

In truth, Tara kept asking herself the same thing. She was still mad at them but she hoped they weren't worried to death about her.

"They deserve to be punished," she told Janet.

"All parents deserve to be tortured."

"I mean, I feel like my whole life at home, my family — it's all a big lie."

"You don't have it so bad."

"I know, but I just can't believe they would do this to me."

"They didn't do it to *you*. They just did it. Go home. Say you're sorry. Explain that it was the thing with the old lady dying."

"I'm not going home," Tara said, but as soon as she said it she knew deep down she wouldn't spend another night at Hell's Hotel.

"Then I guess we're going to school," Janet said. "I don't know about you but I have some catching up to do in math and English."

When they arrived at St. Pat's, they walked in through the doors and went their separate ways. Tara was aware that kids were looking at her again. She had always worn good clothes. Her mother bought her anything she wanted. She knew she had established a good rep for how she looked. She didn't like to admit it because she told herself she wasn't really concerned about appearances; she was into more important things. But now that she looked like a bag lady from the street, she felt very self-conscious.

Nothing happened until third period when she was called down to Henley's office. When she arrived, Henley walked out the door as she walked in. As the door closed behind him, she saw her parents sitting there.

"We were worried sick," her mother said, hugging her until Tara thought she would crack in half.

"Tara, you should never have done that to us," her father said. "Whatever is wrong, we want you to know that we'll work on it."

"Where were you?" her mother demanded. She still hadn't let go.

Tara squeezed back the tears. She wanted to scream at them that they had no right to split up the family. She wanted to tell them that she was never going home again. She wanted to blame them for everything. Even the death of Emma, in some strange way, seemed like their fault. This was illogical, but Tara still felt the worst sort of concoction of hurt and rage that had built up in her as a result of her mother going away and her old friend dying. But she could not bring herself to say any of this. "I stayed at a friend's house. I was over at Claudia's. I guess I forgot to call. I'm sorry."

Her mother let go of her now. They were both staring at her, at her clothes, at the mess she was in. Tara knew they could see through this blatant lie. Claudia was never a close friend. And Tara looked awful. There was a story here. Tara wanted them to scream at her, to yell at her and insist that she tell the truth. If her parents really loved her, they would punish her for breaking the rules, for staying away all night and for lying.

"It's okay," her father said, her father the administrator, the mediator. "We know we hurt you. But we're still a family."

"We'll always be your parents. That can never change."

And all at once her parents had changed back into those oh-so-reasonable adults that they had been before. Already she was forgiven for her wayward night. She was let off easy. But she also knew that what was being said here was that nothing had changed. Her parents — *who would always be her parents* — were still going to separate.

"You're sure you're okay?" her mom asked.

"Yeah, I'm fine," she lied.

"You want to check out of school? I think that the death of your friend Emma is a legitimate reason for a day off. I can drive you home before I go back to work." Her father was so good at smoothing everything over and playing as if everything was now fine. He probably thought that they had fixed everything, put it all back to normal. But it wasn't like that.

Tara's mother was looking at her clothes. "Maybe you and I can go shopping at Spring Garden Place."

Tara wondered right then if she really knew her parents, and if they knew her at all. She had stopped hating them, stopped blaming them. In a way, she felt sorry for them. Unlike Janet, whose parents yelled and screamed almost constantly when Janet was around, Tara had the most civilized parents in the world. They could be generous and they could be nice. But it was funny how that wasn't enough.

"I think I better stay in school. I don't want to get behind. You know how easy it is to let your grades slip."

There. She sounded like one of them. Reasonable. Thinking about grades, thinking about the end of the year and academics and how she needed good grades if she wanted to get into university and become a psychiatrist. But it all seemed so hollow and unreal.

She walked her parents down the hall and out of the school.

"You need any money for lunch?" her father asked. A good administrator always pays attention to all the details, he had once told her.

"Yeah. I'm pretty broke." That was probably the first really truthful thing she had said to them.

"Here." Her father handed her a twenty. "Tonight at dinner, we'll talk. We'll work on everything. It'll be fine, you'll see."

Her mother kissed her on the cheek and squeezed her hand. And then her parents got back into their car and drove off. Tara looked at the money. She thought about giving it to Janet, telling her to split it with some of the kids who had spent the night at Hell's Hotel. She thought that would be the right thing to do. But instead, she put the money in her pocket. If she couldn't find Janet at lunchtime, she'd walk over to The King's Palace restaurant and order herself an enormous Chinese lunch.

12

Take a Hint

Tara did pig out at lunch. Alone. Won ton soup, fried rice, teriyaki chicken, almond gai ding and dessert. But after the ice cream and the fortune cookie, she felt lousy. It wasn't just her stomach. It was everything. She was tired and she was still feeling some negative after-effects of the pills Janet had given her. Now she was also feeling guilty about not buying lunch for Janet as well. It was all too much. She went into the washroom and put her fingers down her throat. She made herself throw up into the toilet.

But she didn't feel better. She felt worse. She'd read about girls who ate huge amounts of food and then made themselves barf. It was a disease. But Tara wasn't bulimic. She had only done this once. Yet she knew that it wasn't like her. As she walked out of the washroom and paid her bill, she felt like a stranger to herself. She fell asleep in biology class and the teacher, Mrs. Giles, had to wake her up.

"Tara, you don't look so good. Is everything okay?"

Tara woke up with a start. Before she could get her head straight, she was afraid that she was waking up in the attic of Hell's Hotel.

Mrs. Giles saw the look of fear in her eyes. "Relax. It's okay. Don't look so frightened. You never fell asleep in my class before." She was trying to be nice. She knew Tara was a good student. This wasn't like her. "I must have been *real* boring today, huh?"

As Tara looked at Mrs.Giles, she felt embarrassed. "Sorry. I guess I lost it. It wasn't you. It was me."

Tara got up to leave.

"Get some rest," Mrs. Giles said.

At home Tara didn't have enough energy to be mad at her parents. She nearly fell asleep again during dinner. Every time her father and mother tried to get her to open up, Tara just said, "Later. Not now."

At seven o'clock she fell asleep in her own room, in her own bed. She had dug out an old stuffed bear that she used to sleep with when she was little, the one she had named Beverly. She took it to bed with her and slept soundly, dreamlessly.

Nobody thought to invite Tara to Emma's funeral. When Tara phoned and asked someone at the nursing home about Emma, she found out that Emma had been cremated. There had been a little sunrise ceremony as her ashes were spread on the waves at Lawrencetown Beach. Tara was having trouble fixing it in her head: Emma was dead. Her body was gone, carried by the wind out over the water, and she would never see her again. There was a dull pain in her heart that would not go away. Tara kept thinking it would diminish but it lingered. Every once in a while, though, Tara felt like she could hear the faint echo of Emma's voice, her voice from the night when Tara was scared and she had reached out in her mind for help. And Emma had told her everything was going to be all right.

Her parents were suddenly spending a lot more time at home. Her father was home every night by five-thirty. Her mother was playing housewife — dinner precisely at six, no evening photography classes or trips to the galleries and photo labs. And there was talk. Lots of it. *"How do you feel about this? How do you feel about that, Tara?"*

They were so concerned about her feelings but they still weren't willing to change their minds.

"If it was up to me, I'd keep things as they are," her father said.

"That's not fair," her mother snapped. "Now you're making me out to be the home breaker just because I want to develop a career of my own." Her father would have that look about him. *What's the good in talking about it.* "You're not the enemy," he'd say. "I know we've grown apart but why can't we just stay together? Why can't you become the person you want to be here instead of in Vancouver?"

"Because here I'm just playing at photography. I wish I could stay here but I know this is my first real chance to get serious about something I'm good at. I need this." Then she would turn to Tara and ask, "You understand, don't you?"

And Tara would say, "I think I understand, I really do." And if it had been another woman on the face of the earth other than *her mother* she would have understood perfectly. But no matter how much talking they did, she was still mad at them. Mad at her mother for wanting a life somewhere else and mad at her father for letting it happen. The end of every discussion would be the same. Her mother was leaving soon for Vancouver. It was all very reasonable and civilized. It was nothing like separation and divorce on TV. Nobody throwing dishes and knives, no screaming arguments. Nobody hated anybody. Well,

that wasn't quite true. Tara almost said it a couple of times:
I hate you both for doing this to me. I'll never forgive you.
But she kept her mouth shut.

Tara had a choice. She could stay at home with her
father or she could move to Vancouver with her mother. Of
course she'd be able to fly back and forth for visits.

Up until this part of her life, Tara had always felt like
she understood the world. Things had made sense. Now
nothing made sense. Her friend Emma was gone forever —
dead. Ron, who considered himself one of the biggest
rebels in the school, was running for president of the student council. Her parents, her own predictable, dependable
parents, had decided to separate and live thousands of
miles apart. And then her friend Janet, her very best friend
in the world, was starting to avoid her for no clear reason.
Sometimes she acted like she didn't even want to talk to
Tara.

Janet was throwing away school. One day she was there,
the next day she was absent. Her grades were in the
basement. There was a good chance she wouldn't pass the
year. And now Janet was having an on-again, off-again
friendship with Tara. They were drifting apart and Tara
didn't understand why.

"Tell me what's wrong," Tara finally pleaded when she
saw Janet trying to avoid her in the school hallway. She
had asked the question before. This time Janet gave in.
"That day after you stayed out all night."

"Yeah, what about it?"

"I saw you come out of the restaurant, the Chinese
place. At lunch."

"I tried to find you. I was going to invite you, too."

"I wasn't hiding. You knew which class I had before
lunch. You could have found me if you wanted to."

It was true, Tara knew it. She had not tried very hard to find Janet. "I'm sorry. I tried. I didn't know it was such a big deal, okay?" she snapped. But she knew it was a big deal. After a day on the street she knew what food was all about; she knew what being hungry was all about. And she had decided to eat alone anyway, to pig out. She had decided not to share her twenty bucks with her friend who would have to fend for herself. This, after Janet had scrounged breakfast for them both. She silently cursed herself. "Let me buy you lunch today. I'll make it up to you." Tara opened her purse, pulled out some bills.

"No, that's okay. I think I can cover my own lunch today. Thanks anyway," Janet said nonchalantly. But there was something else going on here.

"You got a job?"

"No."

"You got that panhandling?"

"No. Jake gives me lunch money."

"Janet, you're crazy. That guy wants to run your life. He wants to control you. Don't be stupid."

Janet was angry, real angry. She didn't like to be insulted. "Tara, you know what it's like on the street. You think I want to have to sleep in some abandoned building every night? You think I like begging creeps for change. Well, Jake is not the greatest but he is dependable. He takes care of me and I've got a place to stay. Who cares what you think?"

After that Tara didn't see Janet in school for a couple of days. She tracked down Craig to see if he knew what was going on.

"I've seen a lot better guys than Jake but I've seen a lot worse. I don't know what's good or bad for Janet. I have a hard enough time figuring that out for myself. I never liked

Jake. But I try not to judge people. I mean, he comes from somewhere else. Who knows what he did there?"

Tara hadn't thought about Jake's unknown history. What had he done in Toronto? Why had he come to Halifax?

Tara got his last name from Craig. Jake Sellars. He wasn't in the phone book but information had a J. Sellars on Portland Street in Dartmouth. When Tara dialled the number from a pay phone, Janet answered.

"Janet, it's me. Can we talk?"

She heard Jake in the background asking, "Who is it?"

"It's nobody," Janet said, away from the phone.

"You make me feel like nobody," Tara said. "Janet, you know how I feel about you living with him but we still need to talk."

There as a brief silence, then, "Jake doesn't want me to talk to you."

"Are you sure you're all right?"

But Janet was gone. Jake was on the line. "Take a hint, okay," was all he said. And then he slammed down the phone.

There was dead air. Nothing. "You can't do this," Tara said into the phone. But there was no one on the line to hear.

13

Fired

Dead air. Dead space. That's what her life had become. They all went to the airport to see her mother off. They helped carry her luggage to the airline counter, said goodbye and hugged just before she went through the security check. And then she was gone.

Tara could have gone to Vancouver with her mother. That might have been new and exciting. But it wasn't what she wanted. She wasn't sure she could handle her "new mom" in another city. She didn't want any more changes. She desperately wished things could go back to the way they were. But it was too late for that. So she stayed where she was, living with her father.

He was trying very hard to be nice to Tara. He took her out to dinner, took her shopping for clothes, bought a TV set for her room. But none of it made her feel any better. Her family was minus a mother. "Try not to worry about it," her father said. "You and I can spend more time together. I want us to be good friends."

Working at the nursing home had never been the same since Emma was gone. It was so strange to go into Emma's old room and not see her there. Tara made a special effort to get to know a new patient, eighty-nine-year-old Carrie Brooks. But Carrie wasn't like Emma. She was certainly happy enough. She had a wild imagination and talked non-stop about all sorts of crazy things. Carrie saw things that weren't there and carried on conversations, even if no-one was in the room. Every once in a while she would talk to Tara directly, always calling her Sara and she would describe what she was seeing.

"See that over there," she'd say, pointing to an empty pale blue wall. "That's the most beautiful sunset you ever want to see. Look at them colours and the trees all outlined like that. I love to see the sun go down over the water. This is the life. Good thing there are no blackflies out tonight, Sara." Or some other time it would be a sailboat at sea or a big cruise ship coming up the harbour.

Tara would always pretend that she saw whatever Carrie wanted her to see and so the visits became a sort of game. Carrie never really let Tara talk, though, about herself or her dreams, like Emma had; Carrie never asked for advice or gave any. All she did was invite Tara along for whatever imaginary excursion she was into. The nurses, who had been trying to discourage Carrie from going on about such nonsense, didn't really appreciate Tara providing encouragement. Tara, on the other hand, couldn't see what harm it caused.

Every once in a while, though, Carrie would get a bit too enthusiastic. She'd be shouting about some scene she was watching on the wall and Tara couldn't get her to calm down. Then the nurse would come in and give Carrie a couple of pills from a small vial. In about twenty minutes she would calm down, her descriptive monologue would peter out and she would just stare out the window looking tired and dreamy, but very happy.

One Sunday Tara was feeling sorry for herself and she didn't feel like doing much of the real work: the dusting and cleaning she was hired to do. Carrie was asleep so she wouldn't even get a free tour of Carrie's imagination. Tara was bored and restless and was wondering what her mother was up to right at that moment, four time zones away. She found herself staring at the pills on Carrie's dresser that the nurse must have accidentally left behind. Tara remembered the night she got high with Janet, the feeling inside the Café Olé with the dancing and the pulsating room. She wasn't thinking about what happened 'ater that night. She just knew she wanted to feel different now. She wanted to escape the heaviness and boredom of the job and the depression she felt about family and friends.

Tara picked up the vial, unscrewed the lid. The contents looked harmless enough. How many did they give Carrie? She thought it was two. How many would Janet take if she was here? Tara read the label but she'd never heard of the drug before. It didn't matter. She took out three pills, thought twice about it and put one back. Throwing her head back, she swallowed them, put the rest back on the dresser and went back to work, straightening up Carrie's room.

A half hour later, she was cleaning the activities room when she started to giggle. It was something somebody said about a new TV show. Tara laughed and laughed even though she realized what had been said was not very funny. She laughed until her eyes teared, then she tried to get control of herself.

A frail old man with a cane asked her if she knew what time it was. Why did that seem so hilarious? Tara didn't know. She took a deep breath and tried to steady herself. As she walked down the hall she realized that she was leaning a little bit one way and then the other. She liked the pleasant, swirling feeling in her head. Her feet and hands seemed like they were miles away from her. And she had an uncontrollable desire to giggle. Tara tried to straighten herself and look perfectly normal as she walked past the nurses' station, but she could tell they were staring at her so she decided to go back to Carrie's room and take it easy, pretend she was visiting with her for a while.

Carrie was awake now and already describing a garden of irises and roses that she saw on her wall. Tara sat down and pretended she saw it all. She even threw in some of her own details, which apparently Carrie could see as well. It was a great little game. Until the nurse arrived.

"I thought you already cleaned in here," the nurse said sternly, as if she liked to order around someone from the cleaning staff, someone lower down the totem pole than her.

"It's my break," Tara said, trying to act normal. "Carrie and I are just taking a walk through her garden. Right Carrie?"

"That's right, dear."

But the nurse was suspicious. She'd probably seen people high before. Then she spotted the vial left on the dresser. She poured the pills out and counted them, then checked a booklet that she was carrying with her.

When she looked up at Tara, with a verdict already decided, she simply said, "Let's go."

"No," Tara said. "You have no right to tell me what to do." Her words came out somewhat slurred and sounded as if they were coming from miles away.

The nurse left the room and a few minutes later, Mrs. Klein arrived. Tara knew that she was in big trouble but for some reason she didn't care.

"I think your career here is through," Mrs. Klein said flatly.

"You can't do that," Tara said indignantly.

"I can and I have. Now I'd like you to leave quietly."

A minute ago Tara had felt like nothing in the world could change the way she felt — relaxed, carefree, happy. But now this woman was giving her a hard time and she felt outraged. She stood up and walked to Mrs. Klein. "I don't think you understand, do you?" she said in a loud, aggressive voice.

"Understand what?"

"You don't understand these people here in this place. They have feelings you know. They need to be treated with respect. They need more than just a bed and food. They need friends. They need life!"

Tara wasn't sure where the speech came from. Sometimes she felt that way, that the patients weren't treated with enough respect. She had never really come out and said it before. But now she realized she wasn't talking about the patients, not really, not now. She was talking about herself. Tara stood very close to Mrs. Klein. She had never liked the woman but now she seemed particularly cold, even cruel.

"You don't understand anything about it do you?" she said, right in her face. Tara's hatred rose and she wanted to hit her.

In a calm controlled voice Mrs. Klein simply said, "I understand that I have to fire any of my staff who are caught taking the patients' medication in order to get high."

There. It had been said. Tara felt the anger swell up within her. She saw several of the nurses standing outside the door, watching. Tara turned to look at Carrie, who was strangely silent with a look of confusion on her face.

"Sara?" she asked.

Tara didn't know what to do. She knew she had made a big mistake. Mrs. Klein stood there like a stone wall, waiting.

Tara made her feet start walking. "I'm out of here," was all she said, trying to hold onto the edge of defiance that had made her feel strong and righteous.

As her eyes were confronted by the bright midday sun outside the door of the nursing home, Tara suddenly felt very afraid. She knew that one more thing had screwed up and she saw her life on a serious downhill slide. She knew that this time it was her fault. She was afraid of the anger she felt and realized she had never acted out her anger towards anyone like that before. But she knew that it wasn't just directed at Mrs. Klein.

14

Welcome to the Club

Tara's father was upset about Tara losing her job. He wanted to speak to Mrs. Klein but Tara talked him out of it. She hadn't told him the real story. If she was lucky he'd never find out.

Their time together was often very quiet. He took her to a couple of movies but it was clear that they weren't interested in the same sort of films no matter how hard he tried.

"Whatever happened to Ron?" her father asked one night after a movie, while they were eating ice cream at Dairy Queen.

"He's history," she said. "We ended our relationship so he could go into politics. He's going to be president of the student council."

"Ron?"

"Yeah, I know. Surprised me too."

"How are things going for you in school, anyway?"

"Fine," she said automatically. *Howz school? Fine*. It was the familiar little chant. But it wasn't true any more. School used to be easy. Now Tara had a hard time concentrating. Her grades were really slipping. "No, that's not true," she confessed finally. "I'm not doing very well right now. I don't know what it is."

"I think you're still upset about your mother and me. I feel very badly about that."

"I know, I know. You're still on a guilt trip. Well, it's done. I can't change that. So the way I feel is my problem, not yours."

"Maybe you should see a counsellor. I know some excellent people on staff."

"Forget it. I don't need that sort of help. Maybe I just need a change, too. Remember I was talking about travelling when I graduated, going to Asia maybe."

"Your mother and I certainly haven't ruled out the possibility. But it would use up all your savings and then some."

"What if I wanted to take some time off from school and do it now?"

Her father now looked very serious. "I think it's premature. You're too young."

"I could handle it." Her favourite phrase. She always used to say that she could handle anything. Janet had believed her. So did Emma. Her parents were usually convinced as well. But now as she said it, the words sounded less than truthful. It was a dream, a fantasy, this travel thing. She knew that her dream of travelling, of going to exotic locations and learning the language, getting to know the people, and living independently was still just that, a dream. The more she thought about it, the more she realized she couldn't handle doing it alone.

"I think you should wait."

"Guess you're right," Tara conceded.

Her father smiled. He probably figured that for once Tara was actually listening to his advice. But he couldn't see into her head. He couldn't see the whole picture.

Tara wished that she and her father could really talk. He always said they were good friends but it was never like that. There was always a distance between them. She could never really understand what made him tick, why he was so in love with his job. She and her mother had been close until the time her mom took up photography. Even so, Tara had always relied on friends for the heart-to-heart things: Ron, Janet, Emma. Each of them had slipped out of her life now.

The next day Tara was sitting in math failing a quiz on quadratic equations. The seat alongside of her where Janet should have been sitting was empty. Tara now felt it was her fault that Janet had gone back to Jake. On days when Janet came to school, Jake would be there waiting for her. If Tara tried to call, Jake would always answer and refuse to let Janet on the phone.

Something about failing a math quiz made her feel like she had nothing to lose. After school she walked downtown to the ferry terminal and got on the boat. It was a bright, breezy day on the harbour. She stood on the top deck with only a handful of other passengers. As she looked down into the dark blue swirling water, Tara tried to convince herself that she had the courage to face up to Jake. She'd demand to see Janet. Then she would try to convince Janet to move out and come back to school. The way things were going these days, though, she wondered if she would botch this up, like everything else.

Seagulls were gliding along with the ferry like guardian angels. Above them were soft cumulus clouds on a north wind, dancing out towards the sea. She looked way up into the clouds, felt the cool breeze on her face and then closed her eyes. *Emma.* There was something about Emma swirling around in her head. Something she couldn't quite place, but she felt that Emma was there with her. She opened her eyes. She didn't believe in ghosts. She didn't know if she even believed in an afterlife. But there was something about this old woman that was still with her, that wouldn't let go.

Suddenly Tara felt a whole lot better about going to see Janet, one hundred percent more confident that it was the right thing to do.

Craig had told her where Janet was living with Jake. Craig always seemed to know everything about kids from the street. The apartment was upstairs, over a tavern that advertised topless dancers. As she walked by, she was afraid to look in. On the street outside, a swarm of Harley-Davidson motorcycles were parked. Alongside the tavern she found a dingy door, unlocked, and a narrow stairway. She went up and knocked on the upstairs door. No answer. She knocked again, louder. Still nothing.

She listened to the rowdy sounds of men laughing down below. Country music was playing. She had never been a fan of country music and she knew Janet had always hated it. The music was loud. It was the middle of the afternoon and the noise probably went on like that for twelve hours a day. She knocked again as hard as she could but still no one came to the door. Something told her that Janet was in there. Maybe she had been given orders by Jake never to open the door for anybody. That would be just like him. Thinking about him made her mad.

Tara pounded on the door. "Janet, how can you live here?" she screamed, not caring who would hear her. "You hate that music! Open the door and tell me right now how much you hate that music!"

It was a stupid thing to say, but it's what came out. Down below the song stopped, or somebody stopped it. The men guzzling beer had stopped laughing as well. At least she got *somebody's* attention.

And then the door opened just as far as the security chain would let it. Janet put her face up to the opening. She had a devilish grin on her face. "You're right," she said, whispering. "I do hate that music. I can't stand it. But I'm not supposed to say it out loud. I guess you just did it for me."

The look on her face said it all. She was glad to see Tara.

"Where's Jake?"

"Out."

"Can I come in?"

"No. I don't know what he'd do if he found you here. You know the rules."

"I thought you hated rules."

"Rules suck. Stay there. I'll unlock the prison here and let myself out. We'll go for a walk."

As they walked downstairs and outside, a couple of bikers looked at them real hard, but nobody said anything as they went past.

They walked to the waterfront and sat down on the grass by City Hall. They talked about old times. It was like a reunion. Finally Janet said, "I'm not going to stay with Jake forever. It's only a matter of time."

"He's not worth screwing up your life for."

"Spare me the song and dance. I know that and so do you. Right now this is the best I can do."

"What about school?"

"I don't know. I think I lost it for this year. I might just quit."

Tara frowned. She didn't have to say anything.

"Or I might just admit that I blew it this year, get left back and try again. What else am I going to do? There are no jobs out there. At least you can sleep through most of school."

Tara was hearing the same old friend that she knew and loved. Never quite logical, never sensible but never completely lost, always expecting that things would get better.

"The sooner you move out the better. You've got options."

"Okay. Give me a break. Let's change the subject from me to you. I guess your life is running smooth as silk."

Tara admitted it wasn't. She brought Janet up to date.

At first Janet stared in disbelief. "I don't believe it."

"Believe it. Life has its surprises and not all of them happen on birthdays."

"Well, welcome to the club."

"Which one?"

"It has lots of names but it's made up of members who start out with great dreams only to watch their dreams crash and burn."

"Yeah. That's me. I'm in. Do I get a membership card or anything?"

"No. You get a tattoo on your butt."

"What?"

"Just kidding. Boy are you slow to catch on to a joke."

They laughed and looked up at the sky. "You know I almost chickened out from coming to see you."

"I can understand why. Jake is very unfriendly to people that he doesn't like. You're way up on that list."

"But then on the ferry, I started thinking about Emma again and it turned it all around. Janet, what do you think happens when you die?"

"Ooh, that's a heavy one. Sometimes I figure being dead has got to be a whole lot easier than being alive but at least I know what this is like. I don't know what *that* is like."

"But what do you believe?"

"I don't know. I don't think I go for that heaven and hell stuff. Heaven sounds too boring and the other place sounds like too much punishment for people who are probably already getting punished in this life."

"I know what you mean. But this thing with Emma, it's like she's not really gone, you know."

Janet snapped her fingers. "I've got an idea. You got fifteen bucks."

Tara looked in her pocket. "Sure. What for?"

"Follow me."

Janet led Tara back up Portland Street, past the taverns and the health food store and the Salvation Army until they came to a storefront window: "Psychic readings. No appointment necessary."

"You're kidding," Tara said.

"She's good. Don't be such a sceptic."

A little bell rang as they opened the door. A woman of about forty looked up from the TV she was watching and smiled. "Hi. Come on in." She snapped off the TV. "What can I do for you girls?"

"My friend would like to make contact with someone who died."

"I don't know if I can help you there. Seances, floating tables and all that. They're not my thing."

It wasn't the response Tara was expecting. "Well, what exactly do you do?"

"Ah, good, an inquiring mind," the woman said as she put a colourful scarf over her head. "I wear this to try to look the part. People want to get their money's worth. Here. Sit. My name is Catherine. In the paper, they called me Lady Oracle but you don't have to call me that."

The three of them sat down at a table. Catherine took a piece of cloth from a rock, a large crystal. "Amethyst," she explained. "Just helps me focus my energy."

To Tara it was all starting to look like hocus pocus.

"You have doubts about this, I can tell," Catherine said. "I don't have to be a mind reader to figure that out. Tell you what. We'll do a session. Pay me if you want. If not, it's on the house — cheap entertainment."

"Okay." That sounded fair enough. "Do whatever you do, then."

"What I will do is make contact, through the crystal, with my advisor. My advisor whose name is Garvey, came to me once when I was in the hospital. I died on the operating table and then came back. Garvey brought me back. He's on the other side — 'noncorporeal' as he calls it. Had many lives, knows lots of stuff. Sometimes he can be helpful, other times he plays tricks." Catherine held her hands over the crystal and then closed her eyes.

"What am I suppose to do?" Tara asked. She looked at Janet and rolled her eyes.

"Just ask Garvey whatever you want," Catherine said.

"I want to know what happens when you die," Tara blurted out.

"Wow. Garvey says you don't mess around. You go right for the big one. Let me see, how to phrase it? He says nothing is ever lost. Nothing disappears. The universe is, well, very efficient. Everything gets recycled. Identities merge, shift, memory is collective. What else?"

"I have this feeling about my friend Emma. She was old and she died. Sometimes I feel like she's around somewhere, trying to help me."

"Hmm. Garvey says it could be your imagination. Could be real. Could be that it doesn't matter which it is."

Tara thought that the answers were too easy, too general. She wasn't convinced there was any Garvey involved here at all. She had decided that she'd keep her fifteen dollars. This was a rip off. Then Catherine spoke up again.

"Garvey says you're right. You've been told something very obvious. We can't tell you more than we know about your friend Emma. She won't appear floating in the air here. It doesn't work that way. It never does, except in the movies. Garvey says he likes the movies a lot. The early ones with no sound. He says he once played a piano in the movie hall. Now he's rambling. Focus Garvey."

Garvey focused. "He wants to tell you what he sees in you. He sees that you are at a turning point in your life. It's not just that death of your friend. There was a boy. There is also something about your parents. Is one of them sick?"

"No."

"Then one is very far away."

"Yes."

"Your mother."

Tara still couldn't tell if this was real or if this was a way of fishing for information.

"There is a real problem here, Garvey says. Not your mother, not your father, not even your friend here who has a very difficult life indeed. It's you. You are troubled. Things are going wrong for you. You're not used to it and you keep making bad decisions."

"That's not fair," Tara found herself saying in her own defense.

"Not fair, but maybe true. Garvey says he doesn't know what is fair and what isn't fair. He only knows what he sees in you. He says you are on a dangerous path. Your emotions are out of balance with your intelligence. You need to stop blaming people — your parents, your friends, yourself even. You need to accept the things you cannot change and then take charge of your own actions. Garvey says he's sorry if this sounds old-fashioned. He came from another time you know. But he says that if you aren't careful you are going to be in real danger. So be careful."

With that, Catherine opened her eyes, put her hands over the crystal again. She lifted it and asked Tara to hold it. Tara was still sifting through what had just been said. She had trained herself to be critical of everything: teachers, the news, anything that might be manipulating her. But as she held the amethyst, a strange feeling of calm swept over her. She closed her eyes and she saw the clouds again over the harbour. When she opened them, Janet was looking at her, waiting for her to say something.

Already, Catherine had moved away from the table and was tidying up the little storefront room.

"Well?" Janet said.

"I don't know," Tara answered. "I don't really know."

"Just think about it," Catherine said, busying herself, acting almost as if no one else was in the room. "Anyway, thanks for dropping by."

Tara pulled the ten and a five out of her pocket, unfolded the bills and set them on the table.

As they walked out the door, Janet wanted to know more. "You paid her so you must have figured it was worth it."

"I don't know. Maybe she just made it all up."

"But it was cool, right?"

"Yeah, it was cool. I'm glad we went."

There were a few more bikes parked in front of the tavern now. The music was loud again. The song was "Achey Breaky Heart."

"God, I hate that song," Janet said. "I hear it twenty times a day."

"Good reason to move out," Tara said, only she wasn't sounding pushy about it this time.

"Don't worry, I think about it every day. I just don't think the time is right. If things get ugly, I'm out of here. Or if I can figure something better, I'll take it."

"Just be careful."

"Yeah. You too."

As she boarded the ferry and went up on deck, Tara was thinking about the psychic's advice. She understood the part about getting her act together but as she looked up into the blue sky again, she was certain that there was no danger, not for her. Everything was going to turn out fine.

15

Don't Look Back

She spent a week trying to get her act back together. Much of the time she was alone, studying. When studying was over she read a travel book about Nepal.

Her father had stopped trying so hard to be her friend, which was okay with Tara. There was this painful hollow spot that remained in her life, though. Her mother phoned at least three times a week but it wasn't the same. Tara tried to think of it as if her mom was on some kind of long vacation to the West Coast. She still couldn't focus on the concept that they were never going to be a complete family again. The pain and the anger had all settled in as a dull ache in her heart and she decided, ever so maturely, that she would simply have to live with it.

Janet had stopped coming to school altogether and *that* worried her. She figured it was Jake working his control trip again. It couldn't last, Tara reasoned. Janet was too rebellious. She would eventually explode and demand her freedom. Tara wasn't sure if Jake was violent. Janet claimed he was demanding and pushy but that he never hit her. Sometimes he could keep his control just by the things that he said. Tara knew that part of that game was to make Janet think she couldn't get by without him. He'd keep her self-esteem low and control her that way. Tara understood that creepy game; she'd seen other guys control their girl-friends that way, even at school. But it could never happen to her.

So this made Tara feel like a true loner now, the one without a boyfriend. She had watched from the sidelines as Ron became more serious with Carla. Tara also saw that "Wendy's Blues" hadn't helped anybody or anything — except Ron's rep. The kids at school had a few kicks over getting the full details of Janet's less-than-perfect homelife and made her feel like more of an outcast than ever. And Ron found himself elected president of the student council and now had a campaign underway to drive Mr. Henley crazy. "Grades are ancient, useless and demeaning," he explained in his latest issue of *The Rage*. "People should learn for learning's sake, not to achieve some artificial symbol of their ability." He had written a long, brilliant but crazy argument that actually made a lot of sense to Tara, although she hated admitting it. Ron was proposing a pass/fail system with individual written evaluations of each student. But no more numbers, no more letter grades. He was calling for a school-wide referendum. Grades or no grades. Let the student body decide.

Friday, Tara came home late. It was seven o'clock. She had taken the bus to Bedford to check out a part-time job at another nursing home. She had tried everywhere around town, but there was nothing. She had to pretend that she didn't have experience because she knew that someone would phone Mrs. Klein to check up on her, and she couldn't have that. So it was like starting from scratch all over again. And she wanted to get the job on her own. She didn't want to get it with her father's connections. Unfortunately she was learning that, without some kind of an inside edge, it was nearly impossible to get a job. Once she had a job, a good one, and she blew it. She was feeling the repercussions of her impulsive mistake.

Tired and hungry, she was looking forward to a good home-cooked microwave dinner fresh out of the freezer, then a bath and maybe a rented movie on the big screen TV. Maybe a comedy with Tom Hanks. She liked Tom Hanks' movies.

But it wasn't going to be like that. It wasn't going to be like that at all.

When she arrived home, her father's car was in the driveway. As she opened the door and breathed in the feeling of being back home after a difficult and frustrating day, she heard two people talking in the dining room. A man and a woman. She smiled. *Her mom had come back!*

"Mom!" she called out as she ran into the dining room. Her father looked up as she entered. Tara saw her father sitting down having dinner with a woman she did not recognize.

Her father tried to clear up the confusion quickly and politely. "This is Joanne," he told her matter-of-factly. "She works with me at the hospital."

"You must be Tara," Joanne said, realizing the awkwardness of the moment. She was a tall, attractive woman with a lot of hair. Tara was shocked, but she couldn't even quite understand why. Her father was having dinner with another woman. What was the big deal? They weren't exactly arm-wrestling naked on the living room floor. Why couldn't she say anything? Why did she feel like such an idiot for rushing in expecting her mother. Why did it all just feel so wrong?.

"I called to tell you I'd have a guest," her father said. "I left a message on the machine but I guess you've been out. How was your day?"

It wasn't a question she could answer. Her world had just flipped upside down again. She turned and walked away, went up the stairs and into her room where she stared at herself in the mirror. A few minutes later her father knocked on her door.

"Can I come in?"

Tara opened the door. Her father came in and sat down on the edge of her bed. "Joanne is a friend. We've worked together for a long time. I invited her over for dinner."

"I know I shouldn't feel this way. But I know what it means."

"What does it mean? I don't understand."

"It means that you are getting on with your life, that you and mom are never going to get back together. You act as if it's no big deal. But it is." And then she couldn't stop herself. She started to cry.

"I'm sorry Tara. You're right. It means I'm getting on with my life. I have no choice. I need to be around other people, women included. I need companionship."

"But I thought we were doing okay, just the two of us."

"We are doing fine, but when your mother moved to Vancouver, we both agreed it would be the right thing to see other people, even if we got involved. We would both have to grow, to change and adapt. We both recognized that we wanted to be happy, however things turned out. We wouldn't look back and feel guilty or full of regret."

"But what about me?"

"What do you mean?"

"You weren't thinking about how I felt."

"We talked about it. We talked about it a lot. And we both believed you could adjust. You're mature, you're smart. We thought you could handle it."

Something about the way her father said that made her very angry. What was he doing, accusing her of being selfish? That wasn't fair. Now she felt like a little kid again, and someone had just hurt her feelings. Why couldn't her father understand what she was going through? Maybe she wasn't mature. She wasn't even as smart or together as everybody thought she was.

"Ask her to leave," Tara suddenly demanded.

"Why?"

"Because I want you to. I don't want her in our house."

"Tara, that's not right. I invited her over here. I can't just ask her to leave because it makes you feel uncomfortable."

"Why not?" She caught a glimpse of herself in the mirror, her lower lip pouting, tear marks on her cheek. It wasn't a pretty picture.

"I won't ask her to leave," her father said. "And if you can't come down and be civil to her, I want you to stay in your room."

And that was the end of the conversation.

So Tara stayed in her room and brooded. Joanne stayed for about an hour and then her father drove her home and came right back. He knocked on Tara's door but Tara refused to talk to him. Then she got on the phone to her mother in Vancouver.

"I don't want to live at home any more," she explained.

"You can't just live on your own."

"Why not?"

"You're too young, you know that. You need a home."

"I had a home and you two changed all that."

"I know, I know. I'm sorry it's so hard for you, but I don't think you're ready to live on your own."

"I don't want to stay here with Dad any more."

"I think you're being too hard on your father. I didn't exactly expect him to avoid all contact with women for the rest of his life."

"I don't care. I just feel like this isn't my home any more. I need a change. Like you, remember? I need a change too. That's why I want to move out. You can understand that, can't you?" But change didn't really have anything to do with it. Tara was feeling hurt. She wanted to hurt back. In this case, she wanted to hurt her father.

"Then move out here with me if you want to. I've got room. You'd love it. Vancouver is an incredible city. It's not like Halifax at all. This place is big. It's exciting. You can see mountains from my windows."

Tara knew that was coming. But she didn't want to leave Halifax. She didn't want to leave her school, the kids she knew, the places where she hung out. It would be too weird in a new place. She would feel like she didn't know who she was. Tara tried to explain all this to her mother.

"Sleep on it," her mom said. "I would really love for you to come out here with me but it has to be your decision. Call me in the morning. No, on second thoughts, call me around noon. That's eight o'clock on this side. I keep forgetting about the time difference. Good night, Tara."

"Good night."

She dug out a magazine about Vancouver that her mother had left her. It looked like a beautiful city nestled between the water and the mountains. The buildings were big, bright and shiny. There were flowers everywhere in the pictures and she read that spring started in February. It sounded like paradise.

So many things had been going wrong for her lately. Maybe this was the way out. Go somewhere else. Become somebody else, anybody you wanted to be in a new place. New people, new school. Why not? What did she have that was so great here?

In the morning, her father was making one of his famous omelettes as if nothing had happened. He was acting bright and cheerful.

"Sleep okay?"

"I'm moving out to Vancouver with Mom," she announced.

Her father was holding a hot frying pan above the stove. He turned off the burner, sat down and faced his daughter. "Did your mother talk you into this?"

"No, I decided on my own."

"Look, I didn't know that bringing Joanne here would have affected you that way. I guess you just weren't ready yet."

"Dad, it's not just that. It's not just you. It's me. I need a change."

"Now you're starting to sound like your mother."

"I just think I have to try it. You know I was talking about travelling — Europe, Asia. Well, that's a long way off but this is something I can do now."

"Please stay here with me, Tara. We can work it out."

Tara could tell that she had the upper hand now. Part of what she had said was true. It would be an adventure to move out West. But she was still mad at her father. She wanted to hurt him. "No. Sorry. I've decided. But don't worry, you can handle it. I'm sure everything will be fine." There was an edge of anger to her voice, a thin, sharp note of sarcasm that her father understood perfectly.

He dealt half of the omelette onto Tara's plate, the other half onto his and together they ate in silence.

Tara's parents got on the phone around noon with Tara on an extension. They discussed the situation. Tara said she was still serious, dead serious about going. She wanted to book a flight for Monday morning. Then she got off the line and let her parents run up a major phone bill discussing it, arguing about it, raging at each other, then calming down and trying to be civil again. When Tara was invited back on the line, her mother said, "I'll meet you at the airport. Just let me know what flight you're coming in on."

Suddenly her life was full of loose ends that had to be tied up. Her father would take her school books back. She'd get her transcript sent out as soon as possible. No test in English on Monday, no more boring lectures by Mr. Hader, no more gossip about Ron and his latest girlfriend or latest cause, no more grief about trying to find a job, not here anyway. Her mother said there were a lot more jobs in Vancouver. She would try there for part-time work.

The more she thought about it, the more she became excited. A new life in an exciting city. Forget boring old stodgy, foggy, cold and unhappy Halifax. She was going West where everything was bright and new. Why hadn't she just packed up and gone with her mother from the start? What was holding her back?

There was only one loose end that didn't seem so easy to tie up. Janet. She phoned four times on Saturday. On the fifth try Jake had answered, so she hung up. The sixth time she got Janet.

"I can't talk," she said. "Stop trying to call me." She could hear Jake in the room, telling her what to say. Then Janet hung up.

Sunday morning Tara caught the ferry to Dartmouth and walked up Portland Street, past the empty tavern to the doorway of the apartment. It was unlocked downstairs so she walked up, pounded on the door. Her heart was beating fast and she had no idea how Janet would react to the news. But then Janet hadn't exactly been keeping up her end of the friendship this last week. And she had stayed this long with Jake. Maybe she wouldn't move out. It looked like their friendship had come to some kind of dead end anyway.

Jake had on a dirty black shirt and a cigarette drooped from his lips as he answered the door. "I thought I asked you to stop bothering Janet," he said.

"I'd like to speak with my friend," she said, simply.

Jake looked at her. "You don't seem to take a hint."

"Look, I'm going to be moving out West anyway, so you won't have to worry about me, okay. I'd just like to talk to Janet before I go."

Ashes from the cigarette dropped onto the floor as Jake stared at her. Then he just shrugged his shoulders, undid the chain latch on the door and let her in.

Janet was walking around the living room trying to straighten it up as Tara came in. The place looked like a dump. Jake turned down the TV, playing country music videos and walked into the kitchen.

"How are things?" Tara asked.

"Things are okay. Everything is working out."

"That's cool. I'm glad." Tara knew that this wouldn't be a real conversation. Jake was there in the kitchen, door open. He was probably listening. Janet would have to be careful what she said. "I came to tell you I'm going to Vancouver to live with my mother."

A frantic look came into Janet's eyes. It was her scared puppy look. Tara had seen it before. "I didn't even know you were thinking about it."

"Well, we haven't exactly had a chance to talk."

"Right. So you're just gonna pick up and leave. Just like that?"

"Yeah. Just like that. Tomorrow I'll be on the plane to Vancouver."

Janet sat down on the littered chesterfield and let the news sink in. "I'm not going to see you again."

"Hey, I'll come back to visit."

"That's not the same."

"Janet, what is it with you?"

"I thought we were friends."

"We were. We are. But you have to admit, you're not an easy person to be friends with. You haven't even spoken to me for a week or more and when I call, you hang up on me."

Janet let out a short frustrated burst of air. Whatever she wanted to say, she couldn't bring herself to say it. Jake was listening. She felt trapped, trapped and betrayed.

Jake walked back into the room and sat down on the chesterfield. He turned the TV back up. "Aren't you two done jawing yet?" he said. "I love this video." It was Billy Ray Cyrus doing "Achey Breaky Heart."

Tara looked at Janet. She was waiting for the wall between them to crumble. She was waiting for her to show it in her eyes. The jerk loved this god-awful country song. They both should have been laughing. *It's gotta be a joke, right?*

But Janet wasn't smiling. She was dead serious. "I think you better leave," she said.

"Why don't you come outside. We'll go for a walk. We'll go visit Catherine and the great gone soul Garvey down the street."

Janet was shaking her head no. "Just leave," she said. She looked like she was about to cry. "Go to Vancouver."

"I don't want to go with you feeling like this."

"That's too bad." Janet was pushing her towards the door now, opening it. Tara was standing at the top of the stairs. "Just go," Janet said. "And don't look back."

And then the door closed, and it seemed to take forever to walk to the bottom of the stairs.

16

Long Way from Home

Tara couldn't believe that Janet could be so cruel to her. She was sure that her friend had changed somehow, changed in some irreversible way, allowed Jake to mold her into some other person that Tara didn't even like. So that was the final break and she had made it. She could leave everything behind.

She felt good about it. She felt she had made the right decision about Vancouver. She was confident, full of hope and excitement, right up until the time she checked in her bags on Air Canada at the Halifax Airport and then told her father not to wait around. She wanted to be on her own.

"Why don't we go to the cafeteria and I'll buy you a snack."

"No thanks. I'm not hungry. I'll be okay from here."

Tara could tell she had hurt her father's feelings by asking him to leave. But she was afraid that if he hung around, if they sat around talking like father and daughter, she would feel guilty about leaving him. And she didn't want that.

But it didn't matter. As soon as she saw him walking away, after they had a final hug, she felt a cold wave of panic rise in her. How could she just leave everything behind? Was she crazy? She wanted to yell to her father to stop, to come back and give her one last hug. But he was already out the doors. He was gone.

She had ten minutes before it was time to board her flight. She went through security, where it seemed that everyone was suspicious. They even opened her carry-on bag and searched through it. Looking for what?

On the plane, she sat next to a young woman who said she was flying home to Toronto from a gymnastic competition in Zurich. Tara was impressed at how self-assured and worldly she was, wondered if she would ever be like that. Someone free and independent, flying all around the world for some special purpose. She introduced herself as Roberta.

"What sports are you into?" Roberta asked.

Tara shrugged. "I used to be into figure skating but that was a long time ago. I guess I'm more the intellectual type," she said. That seemed to cool the conversation until they hit some turbulence and the plane took several hard bumps, making the air attendant spill the coffee she was serving.

"I hate flying," the gymnast said. "I've always been afraid of being this high up in the air."

Tara was shocked. How could someone as self-assured as this, someone who travelled all the time, be scared of flying. "I would think that you'd be used to it by now."

"I never really get used to it. It's funny because I always thought I'd get over it. And I don't scare easily, I'll tell you. Put me on a high bar spinning around at thirty kilometres an hour in an arena in front of 20,000 people plus TV coverage and I'm cool as ice."

"That's amazing. I wish I could do something like that. I used to get so nervous at those skating competitions. Some kids didn't seem to mind the pressure at all. I guess they were like you."

"Yeah, I have no problems with that, but airplanes still give me the creeps."

"Then why do you fly?"

The gymnast smiled. "Can't drive from Toronto to Switzerland. Boat and train would take too long. So it's just what I have to do. One of the things I learned in my training. Had a great coach who worked on your mind as well as developing your physical abilities. He said that you never overcome your worst fears. You just learn to live with them, to keep them from taking control of you."

Now Tara felt that she really liked this woman who at first seemed so distant and self-assured. "Sometimes I feel like I could use a good coach like that even though I'm not involved in sports." Then Tara fell silent, feeling a little foolish, like maybe she was about to say too much about her own troubles to this stranger she had met.

"I'd feel better if we could keep talking," Roberta said as the plane hit some more turbulence. "It'd keep me distracted. Tell me about yourself."

Tara smiled and decided she could trust her. She told the gymnast the abbreviated version of her life. When she came to the part about her mother moving out she found herself trying to explain how hurt and confused she felt.

"My parents split up when I was about your age," Roberta said. "No big deal. You learn to live with that one too."

"Your coach teach you that as well?"

"No, I taught myself that one."

When they parted company in Toronto, Tara desperately wished her new friend was going on to Vancouver.

"Thanks for babysitting me on the plane," Roberta said.

"No problem. I'll watch for you in the Olympics," Tara said, trying to sound cheerful. After that she thought she knew where to go but it turned out she was lost. The turbulence and headwinds had caused the flight from Halifax to be late. Gate 90 didn't seem to be where she thought it should be so she had to ask. It turned out that she had a long hike to get to where she was going. And she only had a few minutes. Shoot.

She ran down the hallway and along the moving pedway arriving at Gate 90 after all the other passengers were already on the plane. She fumbled in her bag for her ticket, feeling pretty foolish and out of it. But in a few minutes she was taking off for the longer flight to B.C. No one was sitting beside her. She felt alone, all alone.

Below her, the forests of Ontario and Manitoba thinned out and were eventually replaced by the Prairies. It was an amazing pattern of geometrical shapes: squares, trapezoids, rectangles and perfect circles, as if the people on the ground designed their fields that way purely for the entertainment of air travellers.

And then the Rocky Mountains — gigantic, grand, scary and snowcapped, bigger than she'd imagined and emanating a feeling of tremendous power. Tara had never seen anything like this in Nova Scotia. The mountains made her feel very small and insignificant.

Tara wished very much that her mother would be waiting for her at the airport as originally planned. But she knew now that wasn't going to be the case. Her arrival time coincided with a special three-day photography seminar her mom was taking. It was being run by a celebrated photographer from England, a "once-in-a-lifetime" opportunity, her mom had said. So Tara was to get a cab and let herself into the apartment.

Tara had a hard time lugging all of her suitcases out of the airport but at least there was a line-up of cabs. The driver helped her put the bags in the trunk and then opened the door for her.

"Where are you from?" he asked as they drove away.

"Nova Scotia," she said.

"Long way off."

"Seems like the other side of the world." Tara looked out at the lush green trees, the blooming shrubs and flowers, the snowcapped mountains in the background. "Where are you from?"

"North Vancouver."

Tara looked at him and thought he might be from Japan or China. "I mean before that."

"I was born here," the driver said, smiling back at her in the mirror. "My roots are in Japan, though, if that's what you mean."

"Oh, okay," Tara said, realizing that she had assumed he had immigrated to Canada just because he looked Asian.

"No problem."

Her mother's apartment was not far from downtown Vancouver. The key was right where her mother had promised. She let herself in and stood there alone trying to get adjusted. Nothing about the place looked even remotely familiar — except for a couple of the photographs on the wall, one of the three of them, her family. She walked over to it and placed her hands on the frame. And suddenly she found herself crying.

When her mother finally arrived, they embraced. Tara felt better; she felt safe now. Her mother was there. This was her new family, the two of them.

"You're going to love it here. I know you are."

"I'm sure I will," Tara said.

"How's your father taking this?"

"You know him — always cool, always reasonable."

"That's your father."

Her mother was looking at the four suitcases. "I didn't know where to put these," Tara said. "I didn't know which room was mine. There are about four more boxes being shipped out here. Dad said they'd be here in about a week."

Now Tara's mother looked a little embarrassed. She looked at the luggage. "You know, when I rented this place, I wasn't really expecting to have anyone else living here. It's kind of small. An apartment isn't exactly the same as our big old house. I guess I could move my photography equipment out of that room over there. I've got a dark room set up and everything."

Tara understood what was happening here. Her mother had already got on with her plans. This business of taking pictures was now an important part of her life. The dark room where she could develop photographs was probably part of her dream. And now here was her daughter wanting that room.

"I guess I was thinking you could sleep here," her mother said. "It's one of those sofas that folds out into a bed. I'll admit it's not real comfortable but ..."

"But it'll be okay," Tara completed the sentence, realizing that this scene felt all wrong. She wouldn't have her own room, she'd be in the way. She'd be living in the living room. Either that or she'd be invading the dark room, taking over and barging in on her mother's dream.

Tara's mother could see the worry in her daughter's face. "Look, you've had a long trip. Don't worry about anything. Give yourself time to adjust. Have you had any dinner?

"No, but I had two lunches. I guess if you time it just right, you could just keep eating lunch over and over if you flew around the world. A nonstop feast."

It seemed odd that an image of Janet popped into her head just then. It had to do with food. Janet was always scrounging for food. She would have thought it was the greatest thing to end up with two lunches on two separate flights west. And up until the night Tara had spent at Hell's Hotel, she had hardly ever even thought about food, or money for food. Neither one. Both had always just been there.

"Lucky you," her mother said. "But I forgot, right now it's getting late in Nova Scotia. You must be tired. Stay in my bedroom tonight. I'll sleep out here. Get some rest."

The adrenalin rush of being in a new place was starting to fade. Tara realized that she was tired, real tired. She got ready for bed and sat down with her mother who started to rattle on about what a wonderful day she had in this photography course, blah, blah, blah. Tara couldn't really relate to it but she thought it was cool that her mom was so happy in her new life.

When she went to bed and snuggled under the covers, she listened to the noise of the traffic and the people on the street. These big city noises would be there all the time. She put the pillow over her head, tried to go to sleep but remembered her conversation with the gymnast, stuff about adjusting to new situations and about fear. Tara tried to define for herself exactly how she felt. It was one of her little habits from childhood. How am I doing? I'm doing fine. Everything is great. But there was too much in her life that was unsettled. How could she have thought that change was a good thing? She hated change. Why couldn't everything have stayed exactly as it was? There was a word for the emotion she was feeling and the word was homesick. The only problem was that Tara knew that home wasn't just a place, it was a time as well. Turn the clock back one year; she had a father, a mother, a crazy but loyal friend and even a guy she was going with who she thought was pretty great. She was homesick for all that. And wondering how she could go back in time.

17

Out of Sync in Vancouver

It was Tuesday morning and she was waking up in a strange room, wondering why the sun wasn't coming up. Then she remembered the time zone thing. Eight o'clock in Nova Scotia, four o'clock in B.C. She had at least three hours to lie there and contemplate her new life, convince herself that she made the right decision.

When seven o'clock rolled around, she heard her mom get up so she did too. The difficult task of adjusting to Vancouver was just beginning. Maybe it would have been easier if she'd had a few days to just relax and settle in, get adjusted to the new time zone, the new environment, the new everything. But her mother was busy — busy with her new life and she didn't want to "lose the momentum" that she said she had going. She hoped Tara didn't mind going with her to the high school first thing and get set up to start classes.

Her mother didn't have a car so they walked the five blocks. The principal was a woman and she and her mom seemed to be on the same wavelength. There would have to be transcripts and papers filled out but, hey, no problem.

They could handle that later. Tara could just start attending classes today.

Tara thought it was too simple, too easy.

"This is the West Coast," the principal said. "We're a little more casual about things. I hate all that uptight bureaucratic red tape that some schools go in for."

Tara was starting to see the up side of the situation. This was a different world out here. The principal didn't even talk like a principal. She insisted that her mom call her by her first name.

In the hallway, her mother said, "I told you, you're going to like this place. In Nova Scotia everything is just, well, traditional. Here people have a different attitude."

"Even school principals, it looks like," Tara answered.

Then her mom was gone, off to her photo course and later to meet with a gallery owner about displaying her photographs. Trying to keep up the momentum.

Kids were looking at her. She expected that. *New kid in town.* She could handle it. The school played music on the P.A. between classes — not just oldies, but recent stuff. The kids all looked like they were dressed in the latest gear and Tara felt a little out of it. She was thinking that in this crowd Janet would fit right in. No one would even notice her. Maybe Janet should have moved to the West Coast. *Stop thinking about Janet,* she told herself. *She's out of your life.*

But what *was* her life now? Who was the new Tara going to be?

She had a hard time finding her classes but everyone was helpful when she asked. All the teachers looked at the note from the principal and were very casual about it. Fortunately, nobody made her stand up and introduce herself. She figured that's what they would have done back at St. Pat's. Here, it seemed everyone was chilled about everything. Tomorrow she would dress differently and that would probably cover it. No one would even look twice at her. She wanted to fit right in.

At lunch, she was sitting alone when a girl named Donna introduced herself. "Mind if I sit here? I'm tired of eating my lunch with goofs." She nodded to a table full of guys and girls who looked like they had just been beamed back from the twenty-first century.

"I like to be with goofs 'cause they know where to score, where to get it cheap. But in school, they just drag you down. You know what I'm sayin'?"

"Yeah, I guess."

"You get high?"

"Sometimes."

Donna laughed. "Only part-time, right?" she laughed.

"Part-time. Right." Twice to be exact. She'd liked the buzz both times but she had decided it hadn't been worth it.

"I know, you're new. I'm making you uncomfortable. Where ya from?"

"Halifax."

"Excellent. I hear they have major music."

"Major. Ever hear of a band called Good Idea Gone Bad?"

"No."

"Oh, well, they're good. I saw them once. Very decent."

"I like music. I talked to the lead singer of Hardhead once. He told me he liked my tattoo?"

"You have a tattoo?"

"I'd show you but it's in a place I probably shouldn't be exposing in school."

Tara didn't know what to say. "Too bad that guy who played guitar in Bone Music committed suicide."

"You gotta know when to stop pushing yourself over the line. He just forgot how to relax and have fun."

"I thought it had something to do with the drugs. What was he doing, heroin?"

"Nah. It wasn't the drugs. The only people who get messed up on drugs are the ones who have big problems to begin with."

Tara now got the picture that she was hanging out with a kid that was probably a serious user of something. She wondered if she should just cut the conversation short and be gone but it was good to have someone to talk to.

"What do you do after school?" Donna said.

"Don't know. I'm new, remember?"

"I'll catch you out front after school's over, show you the street."

Tara almost said no, almost registered in her brain that Donna was trouble with a capital T but then she remembered that her best friend for a long time had been a girl that most other kids treated like a leper.

"Sure," Tara said.

The bell didn't ring at the end of school. Somebody in the office just put on a rap song called, "The Essential Self" by Mind Over Matter. Donna was in front of the school, hanging with a couple of long-haired guys.

"This is Lyle and Dave."

Lyle and Dave had been sitting at the table of goofs at lunchtime, the table Donna was trying to avoid. But then, like she said, after school goofs became her favourite people to hang with. Lyle and Dave nodded and smiled. Lyle was not bad looking but they both had a kind of droopy nonchalance about them. Or maybe they were just shy. Then again, maybe they were just goofs.

They walked together down a street filled with little pawn shops and boutiques and weird little specialty stores selling jewellery, leather and magazines. They stopped in front of a shop that sold nothing but knives and martial arts weapons so that Lyle and Dave could ogle the stuff in the window.

"I keep telling them, little boys shouldn't play with knives," Donna said to Tara. "But I guess they'll never learn."

The two guys laughed at that. They thought it sounded pretty humorous and Tara tried to place the sound of their laughter. It sure sounded familiar. Then it sank in. *Beavis and Butthead.* Probably Lyle and Dave's two biggest heroes.

They gave up looking at knives and walked on. "We're gonna drop by Lyle's brother's place for a little bit," Donna said. "Listen to some tunes, maybe see what's happening."

Tara realized that she was feeling tired. Jet lag. Maybe she should go home. But she didn't feel like going back to her mother's apartment. With no bedroom and no real privacy there, it would always be her *mother's* place, not hers. She would always just feel like a guest. They walked on. The street was alive with crazy people in all sorts of clothes. Tattoos and piercing was obviously a big thing in this city. It was like every third person on the street, this street anyway, had a big surprise if you looked close enough.

Lyle's brother's apartment was pretty beat looking. The place had not been cleaned in weeks. Empty beer cans, pizza boxes, cereal boxes and chip bags were tossed around. The sofa was missing legs and looked like it had been involved in a small forest fire at some point. There was a lamp on, minus a lamp shade, and the blinds were pulled all the way down. Music was blasting from a CD player.

Donna introduced Tara but Tara just kept her mouth shut. Lyle's brother pulled out some kind of smoking gear, a small container of something, a metal spoon and a small propane torch. Tara didn't like the look of it. She had already figured that these guys probably smoked some weed or something but this looked like serious stuff.

Donna could tell Tara was feeling nervous. "Never done base before?"

She shook her head no.

"It's cocaine, mixed with some stuff. Then you got to heat it up. Called Freebase. All you need is one good hit and you're wasted."

So this is why the goofs were so fun to hang out with after school. Janet had pushed Tara's limits of acceptance before but this was different. She had been in Vancouver for just one day and already she had fallen in with a bunch of serious coke freaks. Lyle's brother was lighting the torch. He was pretty loose with the thing. No wonder the sofa had seen some serious fire damage.

Tara wanted to get up and leave.

"You want a hit?" Donna asked her.

"No."

"Good move. Keep your head clear." Donna was trying to hold her breath after taking a hit off the pipe. At least she wasn't trying to pressure her into getting high.

One part of Tara was scared to death but another part of her thought this dangerous scene was cool. She didn't have to get high. She was just there with these crazy Vancouver kids in this totally bizarre scene. *If only the kids back at St. Pat's could see me now,* she thought. *Or better still — if only my father could see me here. And my mother too. Then they'd feel bad about breaking up the family. Look what they are turning me into.*

The smell was really weird in the room. She felt like she was getting a little high just being around the smoke. She didn't really know much about cocaine or this thing called freebase. It seemed to her a lot like what she'd read about — people doing crack cocaine and going completely out of their minds.

The guy named Dave had been sitting beside her. He hadn't touched the pipe when it went around. Tara had thought maybe he was into being straight, like her, just liked to hang around when other people got high.

Now he touched her on the shoulder. She turned her head to see that he had an elastic band around his leg. He had his shoe off and was sticking a hypodermic needle into the skin between his toes. He was pushing the plunger on the syringe and there was a bright red drip of blood where the needle entered the skin. When Dave noticed that Tara was watching, he finished, pulled out the needle and held it up in the air, offering it to Tara. Dave just said, "I got more if you wanna try it. Good stuff. Not cut or anything."

The sight of the needle and the drop of blood was enough to make her feel like she was going to pass out. She tried to stand up but fell onto Donna, then got her bearings. Everyone was looking at her in a curious way. *What's the problem?*

Tara took a deep breath, tried to act cool, tried to reduce the panic building up inside her. "Gotta go," she said, as nonchalantly as she could muster.

"Later," Donna said.

But as she walked out of the apartment and onto the street she decided there would be no later. Donna and the goofs would not be part of her world. There would never be a time that she'd get into that scene.

Tara didn't tell her mother where she'd been after school. Her mother was all aglow about her course and her meeting with the gallery owners who were eager to exhibit some of her framed photographs. "At one place they said I might get three hundred dollars for a single print. How was school?"

"Okay," Tara answered.

"Anything interesting happen?"

"You know. Nothing much. It was pretty boring, most of it."

"But you liked it okay?"

"I like the school," she said.

That night her father called and talked to her for half an hour. "I miss you, Tara. But I'm glad you're with your mother. You think it's going to work out there?"

"Yeah, I think so." Tara decided not to tell her father about the sleeping accommodations. She knew he'd be angry at her mom if it turned out his daughter was stuck in the living room while the second bedroom was used to develop photographs.

"Meet any new friends?"

"Some."

"What are they like?" A dumb parent question if ever there was one.

"They're very nice," she said. "Very generous." She imagined giving a true description of Donna and the goofs. She imagined describing the scene at Dave's brother's apartment.

That night, Tara heard shouting in the streets. She heard glass breaking, people screaming. She got up and woke up her mother. "Shouldn't we call the police or something?"

"I'm afraid it won't do much good. Every once in a while you hear that around here. I don't much like it either, but you'll get used to it. Vancouver's a big city, remember?"

So this was all part of life in the big city.

For the rest of the week she avoided Donna. Donna took the hint after the third time she was snubbed and called Tara a snob. It hurt a little but Tara decided it was better than getting in with Donna's crowd. The only problem was that Tara was having a not-so-great time getting to know anyone else. And Donna turned out to have the biggest mouth on high school campus. First she had told everyone about Tara being at Dave's brother's — and everyone knew what went on there. Second, Donna started talking up the fact that the new kid was a snob — very much into her school work, very preppy and very pretentious.

The labels stuck hard and fast and it seemed that no one wanted to find out if the situation was otherwise. Tara found herself turning into a real loner. Where once she tried to start up conversation with kids she didn't know, now she found herself just not bothering. Ten days after her visit to the drug den, Dave's brother got busted. This started up a rumour that Tara was responsible for blowing the whistle.

In truth, she had considered phoning the cops, anonymously. She knew these were not just kids getting kicks from something harmless. These were serious drug users who might end up like that guy from Bone Music. She had thought it might be the right thing to do but she had felt unsure of herself here in Vancouver. She could never bring herself to get on the phone.

But everyone had known about Donna and the goofs and where they went. It was inevitable. And now Tara found herself shunned even more. What kind of a crazy, mixed up place was this anyway?

After two weeks in Vancouver, life had grown worse, not better. Her mother knew she was unhappy and took her for a walk through Stanley Park. The trees were huge and the forest was so beautiful with the sunlight filtering down from three-hundred-year-old Douglas Fir trees. There were ferns that were taller than her. Along the shoreline, she could see whales off in the distance, dolphins closer in. The totem poles were like something out of a dream. She loved the smell of the forest, the feel of walking along the shoreline and the paths that led deep, deep into the forest like in some fairy tale story. It was in such contrast to the life she had been introduced to by Donna, the city life of kids in Vancouver.

"Give it time," her mother said as they walked beneath the canopy of green.

"I feel as if I don't belong here."

"But look at how beautiful it is. There's no other place quite like this on earth."

"Yeah," Tara said. "Maybe I'd be happier living in a cabin in the middle of a rain forest with trees like this. That I could handle."

Tara's mother didn't know if she should take her seriously. "You think you'd really like to live in the woods?"

"I don't know. I just know that things aren't easy."

"You used to be good at making friends. What's the problem?"

It wasn't really true. Tara had never really been good making friends. She had Ron and she had known Janet for such a long time. Ron had been attracted to her because she was smart and always a bit on the outside, not just a follower. And Janet — well, they had just hit it off when they were in grade six. Each knew there was something different about them, and that had been enough to get things going. "Maybe I could just transfer. I think I'm having a hard time because of the school. The kids just don't like me."

"But the principal seemed so nice."

"She is nice. And they play music instead of ringing those annoying bells between classes, but I think I'd be better off some place a little more ..." she groped for a word, an unlikely one. "A place more traditional."

Tara's mother was truly surprised. "I never thought I'd hear you say that."

"Sorry."

"It's okay. It's not your fault. But can we talk about it?"

"Sure. We can both talk to your principal, see what she thinks. I'm sure she'll be very open and helpful. You've only been there a couple of weeks. You haven't really settled in. So it might be just as easy to try another school. There are a lot of high schools in the city. You can take the bus."

Tara and her mother sat on a large boulder by the shore and looked back towards the skyline of the city that reminded her of one of those martial arts weapons she had seen in the store window. She wasn't sure she wanted to live with long bus rides through the city. Not this city. In Halifax she had always felt at home, safe. The only time she had felt otherwise was that one legendary and horrifying night she'd spent away from home with Janet. But Vancouver was different, just too different. She'd never been a scaredy cat, almost never afraid of anything.

But now, when she went to her locker or when she saw one of Donna's friends staring at her or when she woke up in the middle of the night and heard a bottle break on the street, she had to admit she felt scared. The girl who had always said she could handle anything was realizing that she spent a lot of her life uncertain, uncomfortable and even afraid.

18

Inferno at Hell's Hotel

There were nights when Tara found herself sitting alone in her mother's apartment. She was getting used to it. She realized that her social life had bottomed out. Maybe things would be better if she could transfer to a new school. The principal had convinced her to stick around for another week but nothing had improved. What kind of life, anyway, was it to go running from one school to another for the rest of her life every time something went wrong?

Unlike Tara, her mom had this busy social life. What was it tonight? An avant garde quartet or an opening at an art gallery? *Keeping up the momentum.* Sure, she'd invited Tara to go but Tara didn't want to hang out with a bunch of artsy adults. No way. She was beginning to wonder if she'd be happier hanging out with Donna and the goofs. At least they laughed a lot. What would they be up to tonight? Dangerous fun, probably. If they weren't all in jail.

She thought about putting on her jacket and just going out on the streets, just hanging out. She'd probably meet somebody. But the Vancouver streets at night seemed pretty bizarre. In the day, it all seemed so friendly, but at night — screams, broken bottles, police sirens. Tara didn't think she was ready to be out there alone.

Alone. The word haunted her. Just her and Muchmusic again. Not much of a date. There was that guy again on TV. That writer with another weird poetry video: sitting with a steering wheel in a field of flowers, drinking from a can of motor oil, playing guitar in a junkyard. She remembered the last time she had seen this video on Much. Her living room. Home. Ron was with her. Ron looked pretty good to her in retrospect. Maybe she should have been nicer to him, more supportive about his newspaper. Maybe she'd made a mistake. Maybe she made a lot of mistakes.

She watched music videos until she felt mind-dead. Checked the clock. Midnight. Her mom wasn't home yet. She was beginning to see that her mother really did have a whole new life here. Nonstop activity. She switched to the CBC News. If Tara was going to get to sleep she figured the only way to do it was to watch the CBC News.

Death and destruction in Bosnia. People fighting in the streets in South Africa. Canadians worrying about Quebec separation. The prime minister discussing the economy. That was the one that had her close to comatose. Ready to nod.

"This just in. Dramatic footage of a fire in Halifax tonight."

Halifax. Tara returned from zombieland, her eyes wide open.

"An abandoned building in downtown Halifax caught fire tonight and is still burning."

The image on the screen was unmistakeable. Hell's Hotel. Burning. Completely out of control. Flames were shooting high into the sky.

"Firemen are pouring water onto it but have refused to enter the building, saying that it is too unsafe."

A reporter came on from Halifax. He was a half block away from the fire, held back by a line set up by police.

"As you can see, the flames reach high up into the night sky. The building itself has been commonly known as Hell's Hotel because it has been a favoured shelter by local kids living on the street. It's possible that someone in the building accidentally or intentionally set the fire you now see."

Behind the reporter, the police were holding back a small group of angry kids. Tara thought she recognized the girl named Connie and maybe Charlotte's Web in the crowd. "You gotta go in there!" someone was shouting at the firemen. "People are still inside!"

The reporter took the cue and pushed the microphone towards one of the firemen who was near the police line. "What about that? Are you certain there is no one inside?"

The fireman looked at the camera, then away. "It's been decided that no one will go inside. The structure was unsafe before the fire. Now it's simply impossible. We don't know for certain if anyone is in there. We would be risking the lives of our men. Under these circumstances that would be unwise."

And that was the end of the story. Cut to commercial.

Tara clicked off the TV. She felt like someone had just hit her in the head with a hammer. She was stunned. But her head was swarming with feelings, thoughts, images, fears. Her own night in Hell's Hotel came back to haunt her. There had been candles. And someone had a camp stove. A fire could have started any time.

Or someone might have grown tired of having street kids around and decided to torch it just for fun, with them inside.

It could have been her in there tonight. Everyone upstairs might have been asleep. The only way out would have been down the ladder. It would have been up to Craig to be there, to be in charge, to get the ladder down. But the smoke might have been too much. They might all be trapped up there.

Why weren't the firemen there earlier? Why did they refuse to go inside? If it was a downtown bank tower — the TD Building or the MT&T tower, it would have been a different story. If it had been Chateau Halifax it would have been a different tune. But this was Hell's Hotel. Nobody really cared who died in the fire inside. That's what Tara was thinking. A stream of horrifying possibilities shot through her mind. Faces, kids she knew, had talked to, kids who didn't seem to have any alternative other than staying at Hell's Hotel. The very name of the place seemed so horribly accurate tonight.

She got up and stared out the window onto the now-quiet city street. Her mind was still racing but then it came to a skidding stop on one possibility. *Janet.* What if Janet had been in there? She tried to reason it out. How long would she have really stayed with Jake? Not long. None of her relationships with guys had ever lasted. Three weeks seemed to be the limit. That meant that there was a good chance she was back on the street. She hadn't heard a word from her. That had been part of Tara's plan. Make a clean break from the past. Too clean.

Now the possibility seemed very real. Janet could have been in Hell's Hotel tonight. Maybe she was even in there at this very minute. Or maybe she was already dead. Tara envisioned every detail of the upstairs: the candles, the blankets and newspapers. The old mattresses. And where was it Janet had slept? They had both slept on mattresses far away from the only exit, the hole in the floor where Craig let down the ladder. The odds were good she would be nearly the last one out. If she made it at all. The scream of the kid behind the reporter still hammered in her brain:

"There's still some people in there!" Then the fireman: "Can't go in ... too dangerous."

Tara looked for her address book and zeroed in on the number. She phoned Jake's apartment, praying that Janet had stayed on with the creep, praying that she had broken the pattern, praying that she had stuck to her one bad decision that might well have saved her life. After three rings she got the recording. The number was out of service said the recorded message. When she got an operator on line the man said, "I'm sorry that line has been disconnected. There's no forwarding number." Tara gently seated the phone back in its cradle.

Tara felt small and helpless, not six thousand kilometres but a million miles away from Halifax. She and Ron had talked about doing something, not just a paper, but once they had the public attention, they would organize a rally or a protest. Go to city hall. Demand some better solution for all those kids on the street who didn't fit in anywhere. That had been in the good old days. Before things fell apart. Both she and Ron had felt strong, radical, ready to take on the city, the province, whatever it took to help out the kids on the street. And now this.

Tara saw a taxi pull up down below. Her mother got out. She wanted to scream out the window at her. She felt so mad, so helpless.

When her mom came in, Tara ran to her and hugged her, told her what she had seen on TV, tried to explain about the kids who lived at Hell's Hotel. "I have this terrible feeling that Janet was in there."

Her mother saw the terror in her daughter's face. "You don't know that. Don't jump to conclusions."

"Someone was in there, I'm sure. And the firemen wouldn't go in."

"They probably figured it was too late."

"It wasn't just that," Tara said, feeling the anger in her veins. "People wanted to see that place gone. No one cares if a few street kids get taken along in the process."

"Isn't there anyone you can phone?"

Tara didn't know what good it would do. But she would phone someone. She still knew Ron's number from memory. She dialled.

Ron answered. His voice had that sound to it, the sound of someone who had been asleep.

"Ron, it's Tara."

"Do you know what time it is?" he sounded annoyed, ticked off that someone had called the president of the student council at what, four-thirty in the morning.

"Ron, do you know anything about the fire?"

"What fire?"

"Hell's Hotel. I saw it on the news. They think some kids were still in there."

"Oh my God."

He didn't know. Of course. He'd been asleep. How ironic that she knew, on the other side of the country.

"Ron, were there still people staying in there?"

"I'm not sure. But I think so."

"Was Craig still hanging around?"

"Craig is still Craig."

Tara knew this was a good thing. Craig was weird but he was dependable. He took care of kids not so good at taking care of themselves. He would have done his best to get the ladder down, to get everyone out. If there had been enough time. "What about Janet?" Tara asked. "Have you seen her?"

"Not much. She and I were never that close."

"I know. But do you know if she was still living with Jake?"

"I don't know. I don't always pry into people's personal lives."

Even at four-thirty in the morning, Ron was still acting like Ron. How quickly he had forgotten about the glory that "Wendy's Blues" had brought him.

"Listen, I'm gonna get up and go down there," Ron said.

"Wait. Tell me this. Has Janet been in school?"

"Dunno. Off and on, I think. Why?"

"Never mind," she said. "Go down there, Ron. Talk to the kids. See if you can help."

Now Ron sounded wide awake. "Don't worry about anything. I'll get down there. I'll see if I can do something."

"Thanks. Bye."

Ron hung up the phone.

Tara had a small piece of the puzzle. If Janet was showing up for school at all, the odds were good that Jake was out of the picture. He didn't like her going to school, Tara knew that. If Ron was right and she had been showing up at school even sporadically, then there was a good chance Jake was out of her life and she was back on the street. And living in Hell's Hotel.

Her mother had been watching her the whole time. "What is it?"

"I have to go back. I have to go to Halifax. Now," Tara said.

Her mother took a deep breath. "I know. I'll help you pack something. I'll go with you. We'll catch the first plane."

Tara shook her head. She looked at her mother and could see the concern, the love in her face. She hugged her tightly but then said, "No, you stay here. This is where you belong. I belong back there. Whatever happens. I need to be back there. That's my place."

"You can come back after you find out what's going on."

"I know I can. Maybe I will. All I know is that I have to be back there. Now. You've been good to me but I'm not needed here. I'm needed back there."

"Let's start packing. I'll send most of your stuff on later if you still want me to."

"Thanks."

Her mother checked her watch. "Canadian has a flight to Toronto at 6:30. There's bound to be a couple of openings on stand-by."

The sun was just coming up in the east as the plane took off heading first west, then banking and turning back towards the Prairies, towards the Maritimes, towards home. The mountains below now looked so clean, so orderly and so beautiful like something magical out of a Walt Disney movie. It made everything about her life in B.C. seem unreal, impossible. How she wished she could just snap her fingers and be back in the Maritimes, but she would have to wait out the hours it would take to get home. She'd lose four hours in the time change and it would be night by the time she got into Halifax. *Say goodbye to Vancouver,* she told herself. *Say goodbye to that new life, the experiment that failed. Goodbye to her mother and her new life.* They would visit, she knew that. But she wouldn't go back to live.

As she stared down at the mountains, she thought she saw a face in the reflection in the glass. At first she thought it was Janet but then she realized it was herself. After the rushing and rushing to make it to the plane, it was her first chance to try to settle down and get her head straight. That allowed the fear to creep back in. What if her friend was really dead? Then what? Tara had always felt responsible for Janet, bailed her out of a dozen major crises in her life. She had tried to get her to move out on Jake but Janet pushed her away, once, then twice. *It wasn't my fault. I tried,* she told herself silently. But it wouldn't go away. If something happened to Janet, it *was* Tara's fault. Tara had given up on her friend. And now maybe she was dead because of it.

She had no one beside her all the way to Toronto. But when more passengers got on for the leg to Halifax, a guy in a neatly pressed dark-blue business suit sat down beside her. He had a copy of the *Halifax Chronicle-Herald* that had been handed to him by the airline attendant.

There was a picture of the raging fire on the front page.

"Can I see that?" she asked the man.

He looked slightly annoyed. *What was this girl's problem?* This was *his* paper.

"Please," Tara insisted.

The suit handed her the paper, reluctantly. Tara kept the first section, handed him back the business pages and the classifieds. He smiled smugly.

It was the morning paper. The fire was over. Nothing left but char and rubble. The story was still unclear — who started it, who was inside at the time, who got out. Who didn't. There were a lot of unresolved issues. There were conflicting reports. Some said that no one was in the building at the time. Another source said that some kids had been inside sleeping but they all had got out. Others believed there were kids left inside. Fire officials were waiting for the rubble to cool down before they would look for traces of any bodies.

It sounded very gruesome. There was even a quote from a local business woman. "This may be the best thing that could happen," she said. "We've been wanting the city to tear it down for a long time. Now the mess will have to be cleaned up and we won't have the problem of kids sleeping in there any more."

Tara felt her eyes tear up with rage. She crumpled up the newspaper and held it there tightly with two clenched fists. The man sitting beside her watched and when Tara turned towards him he looked very annoyed. Who was this crazy person who just wrecked *his* newspaper?

"Sorry," Tara said sarcastically and handed the balled up paper to the indignant man beside her.

19

Under the Rubble

The plane didn't arrive at the Halifax airport until six in the evening. She knew she should have called her father to pick her up, but that felt wrong somehow. She was afraid that maybe he would try to stop her from going downtown. Now that everyone had read the news about the fire, they also probably knew all about the kids on the street and what life was like there. Tara knew her father had never really thought about that. Now he might react one of two ways: he'd think that something should be done to help. Or he'd say it all sounded weird and dangerous. He might even try to stop Tara from going down there.

So Tara realized she was now in an in-between world. She was not living with her mother and she was not living with her father. She was on her own, at least temporarily and so in one way she was like the other kids on the street. There was one big difference, though: she had money. She decided to leave her bag with the airline. She wanted to be light on her feet. She could pick it up some time later. Right now she had to find out some answers. She wanted to get downtown fast.

Tara hailed a cab and got in.

"Barrington Street," she said.

Tara climbed into the backseat. The driver was a grey-haired black man, somebody who appeared to be well-past retirement age. He turned slowly around.

"You're in a hurry, ain't ya?"

"Yeah. Could you step on it."

The old guy smiled. "You said that just like they do in the movies. I wondered when someone would get in my cab and say that to me. Now someone finally did."

The guy was just trying to be friendly but Tara was annoyed. She had a good reason to be in a hurry. "Please, I'm serious."

He nodded, put the car in gear and screeched the tires as he pulled off just for effect. "You know it's gonna cost you over thirty dollars. I'm afraid that's the standard fare."

Tara hadn't been thinking about money. She didn't know it would be so much. She opened her purse and counted out twenty eight dollars and some change. Oh, well, it'd have to do. She'd give the driver the money when they got there and hope he didn't mind too much.

He was looking back in the mirror. "You're not one of them runaways you read about are you?" There was genuine concern in his voice.

"Not exactly. I did run away, well, sort of. Now I'm running back."

"So you're going back home," he repeated to assure himself that everything was okay. He kept checking on her in the mirror. She looked very fidgety and very nervous.

"You sure you're all right?"

"I'm okay. I just haven't had much sleep."

Tara looked at the man's identification card attached to the dashboard. She read the name: Reese Harold Garvey. Garvey? Something familiar about that. "Reese Garvey," she said out loud. "That's your name?"

"You got good eyesight if you can read that from the backseat. Better than mine. Maybe you should drive." Garvey had a very gentle friendly way about him, but Tara could also see that he had taken her seriously about driving fast. He was passing all the cars on the 104 highway, doing over 120 klicks. "The Garveys go way back in Nova Scotia to the time when some slaves coming over from Africa hijacked the ship and came here."

Tara felt a little dizzy spell sweep over her. She now remembered her afternoon with the psychic reader on Portland Street. She remembered everything the other Garvey had said. And the advice about keeping calm in the midst of the danger that was all around.

"Yes, sir," Reese said, "The Garveys go way back. What about you? You from Nova Scotia?"

"Yes," Tara said. But she didn't want to talk family history. Forget history. It was the present that mattered. "Listen, have you heard anything new about the fire?"

"Whew. That was some blaze. They say you could feel the heat of it from three blocks away."

"Was anybody hurt?"

"Couple of firemen sucked in too much smoke. They still don't know if anyone was inside but when I drove by there about an hour ago it looked like they were starting to go through what was left of the place." He looked back at her again in the mirror, saw the worry in her face.

"What is it, little lady?" he asked.

"I think a friend of mine was in there."

"Oh, my Lord," he said. "That's terrible. Maybe you're wrong. Like I said, they haven't said that anyone has been killed for sure."

"I know," Tara said, but something inside her told her Janet was dead. It was the unrelenting logic of Janet's life. Jake couldn't have lasted. Even if she had gone home, that too wouldn't have lasted more than a couple of days. Then it would be back on the street, checked in at night at Hell's Hotel.

Garvey drove down the Dartmouth side and took the new bridge across the harbour. He went south on Barrington and in a few minutes they were downtown. Tara wanted to be there and at the same time wished she was far away. She didn't want to confront the truth. She didn't think she was capable of facing it. Reese Garvey had been quiet for a while. He undoubtedly felt bad for his passenger but didn't quite know what to say. When he stopped, the meter on the cab said $34.85. As Tara handed him the money, she said, "I think there's only twenty-eight there."

But Reese Garvey was already shaking his head. He pushed the reset button on the meter so it went back to zero. "You're money's no good here," he said and pushed it back towards her. "I hope your friend is all right. You be careful about things. And take this."

He handed her a business card from the cab company. "Just call the switchboard and tell them to send Garvey. I'm not going back to the airport. I'll be around town here. If you need me for anything, I'll come get you. I won't be far."

"Thanks." Tara looked directly at the old guy and smiled. She wasn't alone after all. When she got out of the cab and he drove off, she half expected it to disappear in the air, a ghost taxi manned by someone from the past. But instead, Garvey turned left on Salter Street towards the harbour.

Now that she had finally arrived on Barrington Street, she could see what was left of Hell's Hotel — charred black brick, a skeleton of a building, part of the roof had collapsed and the floors inside fallen through. One outside wall was caved in. Wet black burnt wood and furniture were strewn around. A yellow plastic police band surrounded the site. There were a few firemen cautiously digging in the rubble.

She lifted the yellow ribbon and walked across to where one fireman was digging. "Have you found anything?" she asked. "Was there anyone inside?"

He looked up. "You're not supposed to be here. Get out."

"I need to know!" she shouted at them.

The fireman stopped what he was doing and took off his helmet. "Look, we just don't know. One kid said there were still two people inside. That's all we have to go on. No names, no real evidence. We just don't know."

"What can I do to help?" Tara felt so helpless again. She wanted to do more.

"I'm afraid the best thing you can do is leave. You can go talk to the police if you want but I'm afraid they'll tell you the same thing. Nobody's reported anyone missing. All they have to go on is what one kid on the street had to say."

Tara crossed back over the police line and walked up towards Grafton Street. There were plenty of people hanging around, still gawking at what was left of Hell's Hotel. Why were there no familiar faces? People had come down here just to get a look at the disaster. It was like a tourist attraction. Tara felt like screaming at all of them. Up ahead she spotted Connie, a pretty schizoid member of the crowd that hung out on Grafton Street. She was a nervous type, jumpy, someone who snapped at you when you said anything to her. She had problems like the rest of them. But she'd been around with Janet plenty of times. She'd been sleeping at Hell's Hotel the night Tara had stayed there.

"Connie, were you in the building when it burned?"

At first Connie stepped back, starting to back away. Then she turned around. "Oh, it's you. Haven't seen you for a while. Thought you went away."

"I'm back. Were you in there?"

"I'm not saying. The cops want to question anyone who they think was inside. I don't want to be questioned by the cops. I'm not saying."

"I'm not the cops. You were in there, weren't you?"

Connie started to walk away, but Tara followed. "I'm looking for Janet."

"Janet?" There was a glazed look in Connie's eyes. Hurt and fear.

"Was she in the building when it caught on fire?"

Connie started walking again. Tara had to grab her by the arm, and turn her around. Connie tried to pull away but Tara wouldn't let go. "Was she in there?" Tara screamed.

Connie looked straight down at the sidewalk. Other people were watching them. "She was in there. I got out. Craig got out. Almost everybody got out. Maybe she did too. I don't know. But I never saw her get out last night. I haven't seen her since. I don't think she made it. Now let me go."

When Tara let go Connie walked quickly away.

The Kitchen-On-The-Street bus was parked by the church on Grafton. The door was open and kids were going in. It was one of the so-called luxuries of being homeless in Halifax. The occasional free donuts, free soup. All you had to do was walk in and get something to eat. She went in but she wasn't hungry. She saw a number of familiar faces now. Everyone looked a little worse off than usual. The fire had really shaken them up. A few of them nodded hello. And then she saw someone who could help her. Craig.

She sat down beside him. Craig, who usually acted cool and unaffected, a little bit tough but always together, now looked wasted, totally distraught. He didn't say anything as she sat down.

"You were there, right?" Tara blurted out.

Craig stared down into his coffee. "You know I was there. I don't know how it got started. I think it was somebody down below who did it on purpose. It was the worst thing imaginable. Now they're gonna try and blame us. Wait and see."

"Who didn't get out?"

"What do you mean?"

"Connie says that some who were inside didn't make it out."

Craig pounded his fist on the table and looked straight at her. "I got everyone out. I was the last one." Craig looked fierce now. "I waited. I waited until they were all out. The smoke was awful. Stuff was caving in. I expected to die."

"What about Janet? Did you see her get out?"

Craig hung his head down. "I didn't see her but I'm sure that everyone got out. They had to."

"Connie says that no one saw her afterwards."

Craig looked like he was about to cry. He wiped his face on his sleeve. "It was chaos, man. It was a big ugly scene. She could have gone anywhere. I don't know. She had just started coming back to the place. That girl always had bad timing, bad luck."

"But you're sure she got out?"

Now Craig rubbed his hand across the table in front of him. He spoke in a whisper. "No. I didn't see her. There was too much smoke. I stayed until I had to leave. I kept yelling for everyone to get down the ladder until nobody else was coming. So I left. I was out of time, you know. I stayed until the end." He showed her a big ragged burn on his arm.

"You're a good guy," Tara said. "You saved a lot of lives. Better have that looked after."

Craig took another sip of his coffee as Tara got up to leave.

In her head it was final. Despite Craig's heroic efforts, Janet had died in the fire. Maybe someone else as well. This is what she had come back to Halifax to discover.

She walked down the street to a pay phone. The haunting image of the destroyed building was still right there in front of her. The remains of her friend was probably buried beneath all that junk, or burnt up into nothing that was recognizable. She pulled out the business card and started to dial the number. She'd ask for Garvey. She'd ask him to drive her home. She didn't want her father to come down here and find her like this. She was just starting to dial the number when she saw someone come around the corner at Argyle Street and begin to walk the other way, away from her. It could have been any number of girls. The army boots, the weird, cocky way of walking. Tara dropped the phone and ran towards her. Her heart was pounding. She couldn't make her voice work. She couldn't make herself yell out. Instead, Tara caught up to her, grabbed her from behind and started to swing her around. Whoever it was had been caught unaware by someone and thought she was being attacked. She swung around hard with her fist at the ready.

Tara clasped the fist and held it. It was like a bolt of lightning had just struck her. And then she screamed.

20

One More Set of Scars

Janet, you're alive!"
"Oh my God! Tara, you're back. Why aren't you in Vancouver?"

But Tara couldn't answer. She was speechless. There on the sidewalk they hugged beneath the street light. Tara was hysterical. She found herself shaking all over and she began to cry. Janet couldn't help but cry as well.

"I thought you were dead," Tara finally said, trying to get her breath, trying to push back the sobs. "I thought you died in the fire."

"I was in there," Janet said. "I thought I wasn't going to make it." She showed Tara the burns on her neck and on both arms. "It was awful. I was the last one down the ladder. I was so out of it, I almost didn't wake up in time."

"Connie thought you didn't make it. I talked to Craig. He hung on until he had to leave. He kept telling me everybody was out but he didn't see you afterwards. Nobody did."

"I had to get away from there. I was so scared. I went up and sat on Citadel Hill and felt so sick, so frightened. Then finally, I just gave up and went home. My parents totally freaked, but I didn't talk to them. I just went to my old bedroom and slept. I thought when I woke up that somehow we'd start over again from scratch. I don't know. I figured that I nearly died so now maybe things would be different. But they just started right in on me. Criticising. Yelling. Screaming. Nothing ever changes there. Pretty depressing, huh?" That familiar air of hopelessness came over Janet.

"We'll figure something out," Tara said. She was back in the picture and she wasn't going to back away again, not from her friend's problems and not from her own problems. "Do you know if there was anyone who didn't make it out? The firemen are still looking for bodies."

Janet shook her head. "No. I'm pretty sure that if anybody was left in the loft, I would have stumbled on them on the way out. I just faded from the scene, didn't talk to anyone. So they probably think it's me in there."

Tara had already imagined the horror of the scene over and over on the long flight back. Now she needed to hear the truth. "Tell me what it was like. I need to know. Tell me everything that happened. From the beginning."

"Well, it will come as no surprise that Jake and I weren't the perfect honeymoon couple. I should have dumped him but he dumped me first, moved back to Toronto. I hope the big slimeball falls into a sewer there. Anyway, I was back to square one. Didn't want to move home for World War Three, didn't want to go live in a group home with impossible rules I could never live by, and so there I was back on the street and checking in with the doorman every night at the best hotel in town.

"Somebody had given me some pills and I took them. Jeez, all it did was put me to sleep. Big time. I barely made it up to the attic. Then I found my a space to crash — far end of the room, a long way from the ladder. I thought the whole thing was a bad dream. I woke up coughing. Nothing but smoke. I could see flames through holes in the floor but it was mostly the thick smoke. Everybody else was gone. I'm pretty sure. I totally freaked, screamed for somebody to help but there was no one there. Not even Craig."

"He thought you were already gone. It must have been crazy in there."

"I don't blame him. I probably deserved to have gone up in smoke. I screwed up everything in my life so bad."

"Don't say that. It's not true."

Janet sat down on the sidewalk and held her hands to her head. Tara knelt down bedside her.

"I made a mess of everything. I even ruined our friendship. Man, I was really stupid."

"It's okay. You made a mistake. I made a mistake. I don't understand how *I* could have been so stupid to just run off to Vancouver."

A few people walking by were staring at them now. Tara didn't care. Let them stare. She knew this wasn't like Janet. Janet usually had a a way of rationalising all the dumb moves she made in her life, blaming everything that went wrong on bad luck or on somebody else. Maybe she was beginning to learn from her mistakes too. But Tara feared it wasn't exactly like that. Hadn't Janet said something about deserving to die in the fire? She didn't like the sound of that.

"You think you're the only one who makes mistakes. Let me tell you about Donna and the goofs." Tara proceeded to tell her about how her social life in Vancouver started out at zero and immediately went downhill from there.

Janet looked a little more together. "You really got dumped on, didn't you?"

"Big time."

Janet was almost laughing now.

"Hey, what's so funny?"

"I'm sorry. I just can't picture you with the weirdos and then like the whole school treating you like you were dirt."

"I was an outsider. Nobody knew who I was or cared. They believed what they wanted."

"That's too much."

"What do you mean?"

"No. It's just that you just described the way I felt my entire life."

Tara felt a chill run down her spine. She hadn't seen the connection. She thought she had understood Janet's problems but she had never really experienced what Janet had been feeling. Now she knew.

Janet looked at her friend. The smile faded. "I didn't finish the story about the fire."

"Go ahead. I want every detail."

"Well, I was crawling along the floor in the loft. I could hardly breathe. I couldn't tell for sure where I was going. I yelled, but there was no one there. I'm sure everyone was gone. I tried to stand up but the smoke was worse so I got back down. I didn't even know which way to go. And then I nearly fell right through the hole in the floor where the stairway once was. I screamed but there was no one there to help me. Lucky for me, the ladder was still there. Craig was gone but the ladder was there. I climbed down but when I reached the bottom I nearly passed out. There was this intense heat. I could see now, though, because of the flames. I was having a hard time breathing because of the fire and the smoke. I was getting dizzier and dizzier. I was about to black out and there was this voice in my head saying, *do it. Just let go. Just give in.*

"I was ready to do it, too. It seemed like an easy way out of everything but then something fell on me from above. It was a piece of one of the mattresses that was on fire. It burned me here." She pointed to an awful red patch of skin on her neck. "I felt the pain. And it brought me back. I ran down to the second floor. The walls themselves were on fire. Even the staircase down to the first floor was burning. I kept going anyway. I ran out onto the street. There was a crowd there. Somebody pointed at me. But I saw cops around. I just didn't want to be there. I was so scared. My neck hurt something awful but I just wanted to get away from there. So I ran."

"I don't understand about the part of just giving up? How could you even think that?"

"I just considered it. Like you would say, it was one of the options at the time. One of the ones I didn't go for."

"Let's go to my house, okay? It's not as crowded there now that my mother is gone."

Tara phoned the cab company, asked for Garvey to come pick them up. "Why Garvey?" the dispatcher asked.

"Isn't he available?"

"No, it's okay. I'll send him."

When the cab pulled up, Tara introduced Janet to the driver, Reese Garvey. Janet seemed puzzled but after a few minutes it clicked.

"You don't by any chance know a woman on Portland Street named Catherine do you?" Janet asked.

Garvey scratched at his jaw. "No," he said, "I don't think I do. Why do you ask?"

"Never mind," Janet answered. "It was just a wild idea."

"You must be the friend?" Garvey asked.

Janet looked at Tara again with that quizzical look. "Yeah, I guess I am."

"I'm real glad you're not dead," he said.

"Thanks. I guess I could say the same thing about you."

Tara's father had been calling all over the place. He had come to the airport to pick up Tara but she wasn't there. He had checked with Canadian Airlines. She had been on the flight but she hadn't picked up her luggage. He couldn't understand where she had gone. He was considering calling the police but as soon as he saw his daughter arrive with Janet, he began to understand.

"Tara, I was so worried about you. Are you okay?"

"I'm okay," she said, giving her dad a hug. "Janet's going to be staying for a bit, is that okay?"

"I think that's just fine. Janet, you're welcome here for as long as you like." Now he was noticing the burns. "You should have a doctor look at those."

"No thanks," she said.

"Well, I'm no doctor but I'm around them enough. How about letting me take a look, make sure there's no infection."

Janet nodded okay. Tara's father examined the burns and said, "It could be a lot worse. I'd like to put some antiseptic on them though, make sure they don't get worse. Tomorrow we'll get you to a doctor. You're probably going have some scars from them, though."

"Hey, one more set of scars won't bother me," she said.

"Healing is the important thing," he said.

"Real important," Tara added. She was looking at her father and knew that he understood what she meant.

21

A Crowd of Human Dynamite

The next day, Tara and Janet both slept until noon. When they went downstairs for a very late breakfast the radio was on. Andrew Gillis, the news anchor on Q104 stated that, "It looks like the city has decided to crack down on street kids sleeping in other abandoned buildings in Halifax. Since the fire at so-called Hell's Hotel, a fire that may or may not have been caused by those sleeping inside, it looks like those who had slept there are being told they can't just move on to another location. The big question, of course, is exactly where are they going to go? The city claims there are adequate facilities but then why do some kids still feel that they want to be on the street? It's been determined, by the way, that there were no fatalities in the fire. The fire marshall has called that 'a miracle.'" Tara was thinking just how close it had been to a miracle. Janet might not have come out of it alive. But she closed her mind off to that thought. She didn't want to imagine that scenario one more time.

"No fatalities," Janet echoed. "But where do we go now?"

"You don't have to go anywhere. You can stay here, remember?"

"I know. But I'm still one of them. Just because I'm here doesn't mean I can turn my back on Craig, on Connie and Charlotte's Web, on all the rest."

Tara was beginning to realize that her focus had been too narrow. Just because Janet was off the street, temporarily or permanently, it didn't mean that the problem was solved. "I think we should go back down there. I'd like to know what's really going on."

When Tara explained to her father why they wanted to go back downtown, he agreed to drive them. But first they'd stop at the hospital. A doctor checked out Janet's burns. "Second degree," he said. "You were lucky." He gave her some medicated cream to put on them and they left. When Tara's father drove them to Barrington Street, he said, "I'd like to stay around and help if you'll let me."

"No, Dad. Thanks. I know what you're thinking. I'll be careful and I'll ask for help if we think we need it. We have a few things to sort out first. A lot of Janet's friends don't even know what happened to her yet. Some still might think she died in the fire. We're okay, honest."

She knew her father had a hard time just leaving them there on the street after everything that had happened, but as she watched him drive away, she also knew how much faith he still had in his daughter.

They walked all around the usual hang-outs only to discover that no one was around. Something was really wrong. "I don't get it," Janet said. "Maybe they were all arrested or they rounded them all up and shipped them out of here. That'd sure solve the city's problem."

They noticed then that they were being given the once-over by someone, an older guy. It was the Social Services guy, the one Ron tried to cripple.

Tara walked over to him. "Where'd everyone go? What did you do, have them all shipped to a concentration camp?"

The guy now recognized both of them. "Sorry, I didn't mean to stare. Some people tried to convince me you were dead," he said to Janet.

"Maybe I'm a ghost," she snapped back. She had never trusted anyone who worked for Social Services, even when she had discovered he was supposedly on her side.

"I never talked to a ghost before."

"Cut the crap," Janet said. "Where is everybody?"

"Down at the Parade Ground. They're talking it over. Things are getting tense."

"What do you mean?" Tara asked.

"I don't like the looks of it either. Since the fire, people are starting to complain. Store owners, residents, they don't want to see another fire. They think it might spread and burn down their houses, their stores or half the city. They think the kids are to blame. Police have been trying to secure the other buildings. The old National Film Board building and some other places."

"Where are we supposed to go?" Janet snapped.

"That's what I keep asking myself," he said. "I know the group homes aren't for everybody but there's got to be something. People are going to have to compromise somewhere."

"Let's go," Janet said to Tara. Tara knew she didn't like to even think about group homes. For Janet, the group home thing had been worse than living on the street. And she'd gotten into more trouble. She didn't even want to talk about it.

The Parade Ground was a little park alongside of city hall, a well-kept prim and proper kind of a space where bank tellers ate their lunches. It was surrounded by a high metal fences and had the feel of some place old, English and Victorian. It wasn't a place that street kids felt that comfortable in. Usually, there were too many cops and it was too close to city hall. Tara saw about twenty people sitting on the lawn, though. They were listening to someone. His back was to Tara and Janet. Something was up.

When they got closer, Tara recognized the voice. Ron. The great suburban saviour had come downtown to get involved in yet another cause.

As they walked closer, however, one by one, the heads turned away from Ron to look at them. Craig, Connie, Jeff — they stood up and stared in disbelief. Ron seemed annoyed that everyone had stopped listening to him until he turned around.

Craig got up and walked towards Janet, reached out his arms and engulfed her with a bear hug. "Man, am I glad to see you," he said.

Ron was looking at Tara now. "It's been a while. Good to see you back."

"Yeah. I'm back."

"You should have stayed in Vancouver. This city sucks. Look at this. These guys have no place to go."

"I felt like I should be here," Tara said defiantly.

"We don't need you," one angry looking guy with long greasy hair snapped at her. "We don't need anybody's help. What we need is for everybody to just back off and get off our case. Before the fire we just wanted to be left alone. Everything was cool. Now we got TV camera crews and newspaper reporters all over us and so people are getting worried. They think we're gonna rip them off or be a bad influence on their kids."

Tara knew that he was right. The more attention they got, the worse things were for them. She looked around at the crowd and saw four or five kids she recognized from school. These weren't all street kids. Ron had probably brought along some of his friends from St. Pat's. Carla was there of course. So were Griffin and Dionne. It was pretty easy to sort out the street kids from the straights. And it was pretty obvious which category Tara fell into.

"Can we talk?" Tara asked Ron, pulling him away to stand behind a monument to dead soldiers.

"You're not exactly being helpful," he said to her in his Mr. Know-It-All voice.

"What are you doing?"

"I thought I should get involved," Ron said. "A lot of them are my friends."

"They're your friends," Tara snapped back, "because you like to put yourself in the centre of attention."

"They trust me."

"Bull. They don't trust you, and they don't trust me. This is not our battle, it's theirs. What do you think you can do here?"

"I figured that we would just stay here, camp out right in front of city hall until somebody notices. When they try to chase us off we make demands."

"What kind of demands?"

"A building. Some place for everyone to stay without any hassles, without any rules."

"Nobody's going to agree to that."

"We'll see."

Tara looked back at the thirty or so kids. A few more had shown up. Some from St. Pat's, some from the streets. There were cops around but they were being cool, hanging back. Every once in a while one would talk into his walky-talky, reporting back about the status here.

What was the status here? A couple of guys were picking up stones and throwing them at the fence and at the church at the other end of the square. She studied the faces.

She saw people who looked tired and hurt. They had been chased out of another empty building last night, thanks to the crackdown. Instead of bringing sympathy for the street kids, the fire in Hell's Hotel had brought fear and mistrust. Tara was beginning to understand what they were feeling — they had nowhere to go.

The same guy who had told her to leave was throwing stones now. He didn't exactly look like he was trying to break a window; he was just sitting there like a kid skipping stones out to sea. The only problem was he was throwing them too close to the cops who were hanging out over by the gates. Not a bright idea. Each stone he threw got a little closer. Tara looked at Ron. He was smiling. *Right.*

"Ron, this is no good. I know your game here. Hang around until somebody does something stupid, until trouble starts, then jump in and pretend to be the spokesman, make demands, get lots of attention."

Ron had a haughty look about him. "Something like that. These guys have a right to be angry. I'm on their side. I thought a little support from some kids at school would be in order."

The guy tossing rocks had now been joined by others. The stones were small, they weren't going to hurt anybody, but they sure as heck were starting to annoy the two policemen who had done nothing but stand around without hassling any of them.

Some of the kids were starting to shout insults towards city hall. Bad langauge, bad attitude. This was Ron's idea: *just hang around city hall with this crowd of human dynamite and wait for it to go off.* This would be his notion of major entertainment. Wait and see who gets his picture on the front page of the *Daily News*. Wait and see who gets labelled as an activist for the homeless.

Janet walked over to Tara. "This isn't right. Nothing good is going to come of this." The cops were turning around now. The stones were getting a little too close, the catcalls at city hall a little too loud.

Ron screamed out above the rest, "We have rights too, you know! You can't ignore us."

He would pretend he was one of them, Tara knew, go the whole route until it got late enough. Then he'd go home to his safe and sound bed in his cushy home and everyone else would be stuck where they were. Tara was ready to call him a hypocrite, until she realized that she was almost as bad. Here she was, wanting to do something, wanting to get involved, but she had an easy backup. She'd go home to a warm house. If she got in trouble, her father would take care of it.

"I'm getting out of here," Janet said. "I don't want to get into this. I'm gonna split."

"Don't go, Janet," Connie said to her. "Ron is right. We have to get their attention. She picked up a stone and threw it so it clanked off the metal fence not far from where the police were standing.

A couple of women were talking to the police now, pointing to the crowd. That would be the turning point. If anyone complained, the police would have to respond. Then things were going to get ugly.

22

Street Kids Only

"I'm not sure this is gonna work," Craig said to everyone. It was only a matter of time before he'd have to speak up. "What the city wants to do is ignore us. If we don't cause too much grief, they'll forget about the fire, and leave us alone. That might be better than rubbing their noses in it. I'm out of here."

Janet was also ready to go. A couple of other kids were getting up to leave but those who were staying looked more defiant than ever. Tara realized there was an opportunity here. Everyone was together. That might be a good thing. But no trouble.

"Anybody hungry?" she shouted, sounding a little too much like a preppy cheerleader at a football game.

The stones stopped flying. There was silence. "I got twenty bucks. I'm gonna go down the street and buy some burgers. We'll split whatever I bring back. Anybody else want to chip in?"

Some of the street kids just laughed. Ron looked real ticked off. The kids who had started to walk off stopped dead in their tracks. Food was a big deal. You don't walk away from food. Tara walked over to the other kids from St. Pat's. She knew that Ron's friends didn't walk around downtown without cash in their pockets. A couple dollars here. A five there. Another five. Some were quite happy to share. Others seemed downright reluctant.

She hit on Ron last. He was still standing there, ready to launch into World War Three, only his troops were more interested in Burger King than invading city hall. Tara looked him in the eyes, waiting for him to cough up. He pulled a couple of fives out of his pocket, made a big point of showing everybody that he had put out for the food.

"Come on Janet," she said.

"You two better come back," Carla said. "You walk off with my money and you're in big trouble."

"Oh yeah," Janet whispered to Tara as they walked off. "Like we're going to steal from her. What a twit."

They had to walk by two policemen to get to Barrington Street. Janet was looking away from them but Tara tugged at her to stop.

"I know you think we're trouble," Tara said to the taller cop, without a word of introduction. "But a lot of those kids haven't had anything to eat today. We took up a collection to get some food. Would you care to chip in?"

A blast of static came through on his walky-talky just then but Tara couldn't understand the message. The tall cop didn't pay any attention to it. He seemed very puzzled, looked over at his partner, didn't say a word but just shrugged, pulled out his wallet and handed her a ten. He elbowed his buddy who added five dollars.

"Thanks," Janet said. "That was very cool of you."

The cops tried to look impassive, uninvolved, but the short guy smiled and shook his head.

It took a little too long to get all the food they needed so Tara sent Janet back in shifts. The feast arrived a couple of bags at a time. On the last trip back, Tara offered the policemen each a burger but they declined.

Everybody mellowed, for a while, except Ron. Tara had defused the fury of the crowd. He figured he'd have to wait now until Tara gave up and went home. Then he'd go back to his game plan. There was an unspoken power struggle going on here. Who did they trust most? Ron or Tara? Their own real leader, Craig, would have put his life on the line for any kid there but he wasn't a talker, he wasn't someone to stand up and give speeches.

By late afternoon, people were getting edgy again. A couple of the St. Pat's students left, said they had things to do. This bothered some of the street kids. Ron didn't care at this point because he knew that as soon as he worked up a little anger again, he'd have *his* plan back in action.

The big issue would be night time. Where was everybody going to stay? "Man, we'll camp right here tonight," Ron said. "Right in their face. That'll make them look bad."

"You don't sleep out in the open if you can avoid it," Craig advised him. "That's what this is all about."

"Yeah. But you do it this once. To prove the point."

Tara studied the faces. Ron had maybe ten on his side. Maybe more. The kids from St. Pat's, those who were still left, looked a little less enthusiastic. Tara knew Ron would be willing to follow through. Once he got his own adrenalin pumped up, he'd stick to his plan. Maybe they'd stay there for a couple of days, make the point: *they were without shelter. Do something.* But before long, someone would get riled, someone would get up and throw a rock through a window, or yell at a cop or do something really dumb. Then they'd all get arrested. Then what?

Back when Ron and Tara had been going together, they had played a serious game of chess. Tara was an ace at it. Ron was pretty good but he thought he was the superior player. Sometimes he won on his own. Sometimes Tara wiped him out. Other times, depending on Ron's mood, she'd let him win. She never let him know that she did so, to avoid bruising his ego, but she was sure she was the better player. The scene right now had reminded her of chess. This time she wasn't going to let Ron win.

Without saying anything, Tara got up and walked over to the two policemen. Ron didn't like that. Some of the others watched her as if she had been a traitor in their midst. She talked to the taller one. Ron watched as the policeman said something into his two-way radio. Tara waited for the reply that came through a minute or so later. Ron thought it looked suspicious. He wanted the crowd to mistrust her.

"What is she doing? Flirting with them?" he said out loud to no one in particular.

When Tara came back she looked a little nervous. "Listen everybody," she said. "The mayor is in her office. She's willing to meet with three of us. Only three. She said we can go in right now. If everybody else stays put."

Some just shook their heads like it was a big goof. Others nodded like they thought it was a good idea.

"Sure," Ron said, trying to make his move to outwit Tara. "It's a good idea. I'll go. Who else?"

Two of the angriest guys in the crowd — Jeff and Wayne, stood up. Under his breath, Wayne said, "We'll trash the place. It'll be a hoot."

Tara knew that Ron had just showed himself as a worthy chess opponent. Time for damage control.

"I made the contact, I want to go," she said.

"I'm going with her," Janet said. If Tara went in without her, she might not have found much support from the other kids. She was an outsider. She'd been away. Most kids saw her as a do-gooder and they mistrusted all do-gooders. Ron could play it tough, however, and pretend he was one of them. Most of the time, they thought he was cool. Janet was a different commodity. She had a special status now that she had come back from the dead. They had all really thought she was gone and then suddenly, there she was.

"Forget it," Jeff said. "I don't think a couple of babes should go in there to speak for us."

Some of the other girls booed loudly and called him a pig.

"No, it's okay," Ron said. "I'm going in with them. I know how to handle those big shots."

"You're forgetting the big shot is a woman," Janet said.

Some of the girls said, "Right on," but Ron just laughed. "Hey, I know how to handle big shots who are women as well."

Tara didn't have any more moves left. She knew that Ron would take over as soon as they got in there. She knew he'd screw things up on purpose, make demands, end up getting them kicked out of there.

"Wait a minute," somebody said. Tara turned around. It was Craig. He had been fading to the back of the crowd but now he walked up to Ron.

"I wanna go in too. I think I should be there."

"Okay," Ron said. He knew how much respect Craig had. "All four of us will go in."

Everybody nodded.

"No," Tara said. "They told us. Only three. No more."

"So screw them. We don't have to play by their rules," Ron insisted.

"No, Ron. We do. Not all the time. Not most of the time. But right now, we do have to play it by their rules. We have one good shot here to say something to the city. To say it real and to say it personal. We don't want to blow it."

Ron looked at Tara, then at Janet. "Okay. Let one of them stay here."

"No way," Craig said.

Ron looked around at the kids. He was ready to say something, maybe he wanted to ask for a vote. But the vote had already been taken. The results were clear. He'd played all his pawns and knew there was no place for the king to run to.

The meeting lasted longer than expected. Everybody was getting hungry again. And it was starting to get chilly. A light, cold drizzle had begun to fall and it looked like an uncomfortable night. When Tara, Janet and Craig arrived back, they were greeted like traitors.

"What took so long, man?" Wayne asked.

"Just listen," Craig said. "Here's the deal. It ain't exactly great but I think it's a start. Some of you aren't going to like it but I think we should give it a try."

"If it's group homes, forget it. Like prisons. I'm not going," Connie said.

"That was what she tried first," Janet said, "But some of you are too old and some of you are like me — you've had bad experiences. So we said no and decided to take it one day at a time from here. There are eight empty beds at Phoenix House and ten at Adsum. Those of you who are willing should go there tonight."

Jeff piped up, "They won't let me and Wayne into Phoenix House. We been kicked out of there too many times."

A couple of girls were saying they refused to go to Adsum House. "It's only for really messed up people and we don't have those kind of problems," Charlotte's Web said.

Ron watched Tara, waiting for her plan to fail. "Just calm down. I think we can work this out. Look, the important thing is that the mayor agreed to meet with us. She says she's setting up a task force and any of you who are interested can get involved in some kind of better solution. You can meet back here tomorrow, if you want and get started."

A girl who hadn't spoke before stood up. Her face said that she didn't trust anyone, not the mayor, not Tara, no one. She'd been disappointed in too many promises. "Yeah, I know who's gonna be on the task force. Little Miss Goody Two Shoes and Mr. President of the Student Council. I know how all that sort of thing works. You two will get your picture in the paper and we'll still be on the street with nothing."

"No," Janet said. "That's not it. Tara's not gonna be on it, and neither is Ron. Street kids only. That was the rule. We all agreed that was the only way it would really work." She paused and looked around at the faces of the other kids. "I decided I'm going to get involved. I'm going to do it."

"I'm gonna hate it but I'm gonna do it too," Craig said. "I'll need help. Let me know tomorrow who else wants to be in on it."

Tara and Janet talked to everyone who was heading off to Phoenix or Adsum. Some of them had been there before. Some hadn't. There were about ten street kids left without any place to go. Tara had asked the four remaining kids from St. Pat's to hang around, though.

"What about us?" Connie asked. "Did she say we could crash at the old Film Board building without being hassled?"

"No." Tara said. "She said that the police would chase out anybody in there."

"Then we're right back where we started," Ron said.

"No, we aren't. I said that those of us who lived at home would take home whoever was left." It was starting to rain steadily now, a cold, relentless Halifax rain that soaked through to the skin. In a few minutes, everyone would be very wet and very cold.

"Forget it," Wayne said. He and Jeff had started to drift away.

"No," Janet said, then turning to Ron, "You could handle a couple a guests for the night, right?"

Ron was up against a wall. "No problem," he said, trying to sound cheerful, "C'mon." You could tell he hated the idea.

Carla said no way, that she was sorry but she just couldn't bring home anybody to stay at her house. The fact that she wimped out seemed to actually give courage to Dionne and Claudia who each took two girls. That left Craig and Connie.

"I got a big house," Tara said. "You can both come to my place. Craig, I hope you don't mind sleeping on the sofa."

Craig smiled. "I think I can handle it if it's only for one night."

23

Pulling Things Back Together

Tara's father tried not to act surprised when he saw Tara arrive home with three house guests instead of one.

"Anybody hungry?" he asked.

Craig and Connie acted truly uncomfortable at first but once everybody ate, everyone seemed to mellow. In the morning both Craig and Connie said they had to leave.

"I really like it here," Craig said. "But it's not me, you know. Not all of us can just live inside other people's homes. It's nothing personal. We really need something of our own. I'm gonna try to convince them of that at city hall."

"You're welcome back here if you ever need a place to stay," Tara said, probably overstepping her bounds, but her father didn't try to say otherwise.

After they left, Tara asked Janet, "What about you? I'd really like you to stay."

"I'm confused," Janet said.

Tara wanted to state the obvious. *Janet, you are often confused.* "If it's okay, I am gonna stay for a while. Then decide. But I kind of feel like Craig. There are other kids still downtown. And there's going to be more. I think I'm a little like Craig. For him, the street is like a job, an important one. A new kid shows up and he tries to make sure the new kid doesn't get messed up. I feel that we need to stick together. It's like this: down there is the only place where I've ever really felt wanted. No, that's not exactly true. It's the only place I've ever felt *needed*. Do you know what that feels like?"

"Yeah," Tara said, "I think I do. And I know that I'm different. I'm not part of that world. But I'm still part of your world, right?"

"Right."

"So then we both learn to adapt. Whatever happens."

"Whatever happens."

At school, Ron came charging up to Tara. He didn't exactly look happy to see her. "You know what those creeps did?"

"What creeps?" Tara asked.

"Those two hoseheads who stayed at my house. Those two zeroes that we were trying to help."

"Wayne and Whatsisname. Yeah. How did it go?"

"They devoured the kitchen, then talked to my parents in all kinds of indecent language. Then in the morning, they were gone and guess what?"

"What?"

"They ripped off the VCR and CD player, not to mention most of my CDs."

Tara could see that Ron was saying, *this is all your fault*. And maybe she should have felt sorry for him. But she was rather enjoying seeing Ron so flipped out. "Not everybody who lives on the street is a saint," she said without an ounce of sympathy in her voice.

"I don't believe those jerks. You show a little generosity and the first thing they do is rob you. Forget trying to be nice to people."

Tara knew this other side of Ron. Ron who was always used to getting his way, winning his battles, Ron who only had good things happen to him. In some ways, Ron reminded her of herself a little while back. "Ron, don't be so naive. Those guys shouldn't have ripped you off. Hey, you can call the cops, or better yet, call the insurance company. They probably are a couple of not-so-nice guys but it doesn't mean all the kids on the street are that way. Besides, what was it you said in your paper. We are responsible for their condition. Something like that. So I wouldn't take it personally."

Ron shook his head. "Man, you just don't get it. It's wrong for somebody to rip you off when you're trying to help."

"Yeah, it is wrong. But there are a lot of things worse."

"Easy for you to say."

Nothing much had changed at school. It would be a struggle to catch up in her subjects but her teachers were understanding, Mr. Henley suggested she may have to make up some work in the summer but Tara knew she could probably pull things back together before that. After a few days, Janet had moved out and was back to life on the street. Some nights she would stay at Phoenix House, once in a while she'd go home with Tara. Other times it was an empty warehouse that Craig had found down by the waterfront. But she had dropped back into school fulltime. Afternoons were spent studying with Tara at Café Mocha or the Green Bean or sometimes just hanging out at the public library on Spring Garden Road.

They were walking out of the library one day when Jake showed up. He looked at Janet and just shook his head.

"What were you doing in there?" he asked sarcastically.

"Hanging out," Janet said.

Jake looked at the books they were carrying, then at Tara. "What's the point?" Jake asked.

Tara started to say something, something about Jake that would have been less than complimentary, something in language she saved only for those moments when she was faced with the lowest of the low. But Janet stopped her.

"The point is I'm back in school. The point is I don't need you, don't want you and would prefer to see squirming maggots in my food rather than have to look at you."

Jake pretended he didn't hear it. "Hey, whatever I did to make you mad, I'm sorry. I just thought you should know I was back. I wanted to see you. Maybe you can come over."

"Maybe not," Tara snapped and started to pull Janet away. But Janet yanked herself free.

"I thought you were gone for good. What happened to Toronto?"

Jake shrugged. "Wasn't as much fun as I expected."

"Now what?"

"Well, you know, I'm back. I thought maybe we could pick up where we left off."

"I don't think I got the time. School and stuff, ya know?"

Tara held back. She really wanted to shred the guy, tell him what she really felt about him but she hung back.

"School?" Jake scoffed. "You're no good at that stuff. Babe, they don't want you in that place. They'll string you along for a while, but wait and see, they're not gonna let you graduate. It's fixed. You don't have that kind of smarts up here." He pointed to her head, but it wasn't just pointing; he tapped her with his finger and held it there like he was drilling into her skull.

Janet didn't pull away. Jake had her locked in with his stare. "You know that it's not gonna work out. You're just not cut out for all that school bullshit. You're not that smart. But, hey, I never cared about that. I was there, wasn't I? I took care of you. Didn't matter to me if you didn't have brains. I realize I made a mistake. I shouldn't have split. C'mon back. I got a new place. Nicer than the last one."

It was a test. And a big one. Janet looked at her books, back at Tara then at Jake who had suddenly put on a very convincing puppy-dog face. If you like greasy hair and pudgy cheeks and sideburns like Elvis, you might almost have called him cute.

Janet was still fixed in his stare, like he was holding some power over her. He tried to drive home his point, speaking close to her in a whisper so Tara couldn't hear. "You're not like her," he said, motioning towards Tara. "She's got everything. You've got nothing. Forget about school. Come back with me. It'll be just like before. Only better."

Tara wanted to jump between them, grab onto Janet and just get her away from there. This was all wrong. Jake sounded too convincing. In the old days, this was the sort of scene where Tara would *have* to step in and takeover. It would be the only way to avert disaster. She reached out to grab onto Janet's arm but then she stopped.

"Jake," Janet said. "I got to tell ya. I have a pretty busy schedule. I don't know if I could fit you into my life. School's not so bad. Studying sucks but it's better than having to listen to 'Achey Breaky Heart' at two in the morning. And like, even now, I'd like to hang around and rehash old times but I have this meeting with the mayor in about forty-five minutes."

"The mayor?" Jake asked.

But Janet was already walking away with Tara trying to catch up.

A Turn in the Street

Tara decided to write a long letter of apology to Mrs. Klein. She really wanted her old job back. She missed talking to the old people and her life had changed in such a big way that she wanted to try to fill in some of the gaps. Working at the nursing home again would be good for her. And she wouldn't screw up a second time.

Strangely enough, Mrs. Klein gave her a warm reception. Tara figured that her old boss must have talked with the nurses who knew Tara at work and she was convinced that Tara had been good for the place except for the one mistake that got her fired. Tara would be given a second chance.

"You're no longer part of the janitorial staff, though," Mrs. Klein told her. "We want to see if you can handle working as a social assistant. We want you to spend more time with the clients here. Talk to them. Plan something for each of them to do. Be inventive and use your imagination."

Tara could hardly believe what she was hearing.

"I don't have to do any cleaning?"

"None."

"Changing sheets or any of that?"

"Not necessary. We want you to spend time with the patients. Just like you did with Emma when you should have been cleaning."

Tara felt a little guilty. Mrs. Klein obviously knew she had spent plenty of time "goofing off."

"I guess I always thought that relating with the people was more important than cleaning."

"Apparently so did your friend, Emma."

"What do you mean?"

"Well, the truth is we're not exactly hiring you back out the goodness of our hearts. It seems that Emma left a certain amount of money to the nursing home in her will. It was earmarked for one purpose only — to hire you and one other person of your choosing to spend time just socializing, as she put it, with those living here. Emma was convinced it improves the health and the mind of all concerned."

Mrs. Klein had returned to her old formal self. "I'm not exactly sure what we're going to do about the second party who is to be hired. We must be very careful about these things, you know. The wrong person could cause more harm than good."

Tara knew exactly what Mrs. Klein was thinking. It was going to be a very tough sell.

"So the other person can be of my choosing, is that what Emma said?"

"Yes it is. But how can we know you'll choose wisely? We really should consider all those other applications for work we have on hand. We must be fair to them. There are dozens of young men and women who have applied for part-time work."

"I agree," Tara said. "But I know the best candidate for the job. She has her application on file with you. Janet O'Brien."

Mrs. Klein saw this coming. "I don't think we could bend that far. I just don't think we should do it."

"You don't know Janet. She's had a hard time but she's completely changed. You have people in here who have experienced very difficult lives, some who are now living with pain. Janet can understand what those people feel better than you or me. And she's become serious about herself and about school and well, she's involved in community work."

"What sort of community work?"

"She works on a committee with the mayor and several city aldermen."

"I find that a little far-fetched."

"Check it out for yourself. Call city hall."

At school, Mr. Henley finally figured out a good reason to have Ron resign as president of student council. He had pushed the "no grades" issue too far and, in the end, he failed to get support from the student body. Everybody, according to Ron, was wimping out, "afraid they wouldn't get accepted into university if they didn't have letters and numbers on a stupid piece of paper."

Ron still had a chip on his shoulder towards the downtown crowd after he had his video and audio gear ripped off. Craig and the other kids had become a bit more cautious about getting involved with him. "I was beginning to feel a little exploited," was the way Craig put it.

In fact, it seemed like Ron had completely fallen from his lofty heights of popularity. Carla had told him that she wanted someone who was a little more fun to be with. Ron was just back to being Ron: opinionated, smart, ambitious and a little too likely to talk before he finished thinking. But he had lost the edge of confidence that had been his trademark. And, in his effort to get rid of grades forever at St. Pat's, his own grades had been slipping down the toilet.

Tara felt sorry for him. She decided she still liked the guy, despite his faults. "I want us to do a new edition of *The Rage*," she said.

Ron had let the paper slide. He hadn't kept his promise to do one a month. "I don't know. I just don't know. I'm not sure anybody cares any more. All it would bring me is more grief."

"When did you ever back down for that reason?"

"I don't know. It just wouldn't be the same."

"No it wouldn't. This time, I'd be involved. You never did let me write for your paper the way you promised."

"Well, you know. Things got complicated."

"Yeah. Everything with you is always complicated. But I want us to do this paper together. I'll help you sell advertising space to some of the music stores, skateboard shops and cafés."

"You'd do that for me?" Ron seemed astonished. Selling advertising was the true dirty work, the work that brought in enough cash to pay the printing bill.

"Yeah, I'll do it. Because you're going to let me write the lead story."

"Sounds like you want to take over."

"No. I want to work together. A truly alternative newspaper is an excellent idea. The truth is I didn't really have anything to write about before. Now I do."

"What are you gonna write about?"

"I'm gonna call it 'Tara's Blues.' "

And so Tara wrote her story. She decided it might help people understand a lot of things: the way you feel when your parents break up, what it's like to be alone, a new kid in a big city and even what it was like to spend a night in

Hell's Hotel. A lot of kids in school thought Tara had always been someone who had it made, somebody who never fell on her face. Now they'd know there was no such thing. Everybody has complicated, difficult lives. "Tara's Blues" would testify to that.

The story included some honest, tough language. Tara knew she had to make it real, quote the kids who she knew on the street, use the language of the characters she met in Vancouver. Donna and the goofs weren't the types to speak the Queen's English.

Ron loved the piece. It was too long, too rough, but he printed the whole thing. He included an article about his own failed attempt to get rid of grades. And he included a story about how the city still hassled skateboarders. Craig and Janet included a final piece about what was being discussed as an alternative for kids on the street. The mayor's committee wasn't exactly going smoothly. There were snags. What seemed practical and logical to the city officials, sounded unreasonable to kids living on the street used to their freedom. Like everything else, it was a complicated issue with no easy solutions. But people were talking. And the city council was beginning to realize how important it was to have people like Craig and Janet in constant communication with them. Wheels turned slowly, but wheels were turning.

Tara's mom flew back from Vancouver and stayed for five days. For a short while she had a mother and a father in the same house with her. Things would never be the same as before and nobody was really trying to patch up the marriage. "I want us to stay friends," her mother said, "all of us."

"Some days that seems so hard to do," Tara confided. "Some days I still feel like hating both of you for splitting up."

"That means then that some days you don't hate us at all, right?" her father said.

"Yeah."

"There's no turning back," her mother said. "I miss you. I even miss your father sometimes. But I really am happy at what I'm doing and I should be allowed to be happy."

"I know that," Tara said. "It just takes a long while getting used to you not being here."

"I'm sorry Vancouver didn't work out," she said.

"It's okay. I think I had to go to the other side of the country before I knew where I really belonged."

"I still wish you had consulted us before you splashed our family history all over five thousand copies of that newspaper of yours."

"It's Ron's newspaper," Tara corrected. "And we printed six thousand copies."

"I thought you and Ron were history," Tara's mom said.

"Ron is an interesting person. We're friends."

The next day the two friends were sitting in Mr. Henley's office. "I thought we've been all though this language business, before, Ron. I warned you that you can't go distributing anything with that kind of foul language, those offensive words, in this school."

"I remember that," Ron said. "And as you probably know, we did not distribute the paper in the school. I abided by your rules."

Mr. Henley looked a little flustered. "But you, Tara, you used to be such a sensible girl. I don't know how you could have written this, this exposé of yourself. And I suppose you're the one whom I should hold responsible for the reprehensible language. I'm seriously considering having you both suspended."

Ron was quick to the defense. "That would be outrageous. Go ahead, suspend me, it's my paper but you can't suspend Tara. She has one of the highest grade point averages in the school. If you want to punish anyone, punish me. Not her. All she did was have the guts to tell the truth."

It was true. Henley knew this. He could suspend Ron. Everybody knew he was a troublemaker. Suspension meant nothing to Ron. He always bounced back. Somehow he'd end up using the suspension to his advantage, probably use the time to crank out another edition of *The Rage*. But Tara was another story. Henley knew he would get flak if she was suspended. She had always been one of the best students at St. Pat's. He had a problem.

"I'll accept full responsibility for my actions," Tara said.

"Somehow I knew you were going to say something like that," Henley commented. Sure, he had succeeded in getting Ron kicked off of student council but that was because Ron did it to himself. He didn't know when to shut up. He criticised too many of his fellow students until he lost all allies. But now this paper thing kept coming back to haunt him. Ron had been true to his word. The paper was distributed on the sidewalk *outside* the school but not *in* school. Not much difference, but at least there was a thin line of discipline here. And at least the current issue had not mentioned the VP. Henley wasn't the evil culprit this time. He threw his hands up in the air. "Both of you, get out of my office. I'm going to have to admit that maybe you didn't really step over the line this time. You came close but if you keep it outside of school, I have no jurisdiction. I just have one bit of advice."

"What's that?" Ron asked.

"You're just kids. Why don't you relax? Have some fun. Don't take everything so bloody seriously. We'd all get along a lot better."

"We'll take that into consideration," Tara said as they left.

Outside after school, Ron seemed pretty proud of the way things went. "I wasn't going to let you take the rap," he said. Ron was back into his cool, big-man role.

"I appreciate that," Tara said.

"You know I think we work really well together."

Tara could see where this was going. "On some things."

"I was wondering if maybe I could come over to your place tonight, watch some videos or a movie maybe."

Tara smiled, remembered the time she and Ron had spent together, back when they were more than just friends. She didn't quite know how to say it to him, but she wasn't interested in that now. "I don't think so. I don't know. I'm still trying to put the pieces of my life back together."

Ron was hurt. He had a hard time when anyone turned him down and he was certain that he had just been put in his place. "Oh," he said.

"But let's talk tomorrow at lunch about the next issue of *The Rage*," she said.

Ron shuffled his feet and watched her walk away, his ego more than a little damaged again.

An hour later at the Green Bean café, Janet was waiting for her as planned. Tara had been holding back the news about the job. Janet had been interviewed and then Mrs. Klein had come up with all kinds of excuses why she shouldn't hire Janet. Tara had taken it upon herself to talk to Emma's son and find out exactly what had been in the will. Emma's son was not too happy about talking to her. After all, the money that was going towards the nursing home jobs was money that he felt was rightfully his. In the end, though, he showed Tara the will, and it was crystal clear. Tara would be responsible for choosing the second "social assistant." She had informed Mrs. Klein, ever so politely, that she had no choice.

"You got the job," Tara told Janet as they sat down at the table.

Janet jumped up, screeched and gave Tara a hug. "I don't believe it."

"Believe it," Tara said, "but it's not exactly a career. Just a part-time job."

"I promise I won't screw it up."

"I know you won't. If you do, I'll kill you."

They laughed and ordered. Tara was celebrating: New York cheesecake for both of them and cappuccino.

"You know you can still stay at my house for as long as you like. My father said it was okay."

"I know, I know. But like I can't depend on you for everything. I need my own life."

"I've always known that. But you can't keep up with this street thing. That warehouse might be the next Hell's Hotel."

"Well, the city hasn't quite figured out what to do with us. But I've been checking out group homes. They're all different. I think I found one I can handle for a while anyway. Then maybe I can use the money from my job to split rent with some others for our own place. Something cheap but something decent."

"That's better than life with Jake."

"Jake had his good points."

"Yeah, sure."